Biocide

Denise Kawaii

© 2017 Denise Kawaii

All rights reserved. No part of this text may be reproduced without expressed permission from the author. Any requests for use beyond comment and review may be directed to www.KawaiiTimes.com

Biocide; Book Two
First edition: April 2017
Edited by Ava Roberts, www.avaedits.com

For Sir Robert.

ACKNOWLEDGMENTS

Before I thank anyone individually, I would like to thank every person who ever read Adaline (book one of this series) and asked me if there would be more books. You always seem to pop into my life at the exact moment when I question whether or not I should keep writing. I may never have completed Biocide without your prodding.

Additionally, I am thankful for Sarah for encouraging me through writer's block. Elise for being around through the highs and lows. To Kendra for scattered coffee dates and knowing what it's like to be exhausted and productive at the same time. Thank you to Mom for being supportive of all of my writing, especially the things that she doesn't want to read. Thanks to Ava and Randall for support and comedic relief while we all live the dream.

And to Keith, for plowing through life with me one sentence at a time.

"Despite its moral implications, I've begun to consider Biocide as an option. A method which would be used to exterminate biologically inferior subjects, leaving more resources for the better specimens. We must systematically purify our legions if we hope to survive."

- Father's Journal Entry

CHAPTER 1

    The Career Aptitude Testing center was buzzing with a new kind of energy. Boy 1124562, called 62 by his friends, had developed enough to do more than just learn from lectures and diagrams. He, and the hundreds of other Boys animated in his batch, were being moved to a new compound. They were being promoted to the Training and Skills Kinesiology center.
    It had been nearly 250 cycles since 62 had embraced his anomaly and had scared off the doctor who had tried to stop his ability to dream. 62 stretched his arms out in satisfaction as he woke from his most recent session with his imagination. It wasn't much of a stretch; elbows bent and knees locked within the narrow walls of his cube. But it felt good to move. He smiled up at the ceiling as he thought back on the dream he'd just had and shook his head. Although he knew dreams were an

anomaly, he didn't know how his brothers survived the monotony of C.A.T. without them.

      62 picked up his breakfast tablet and downed it with two gulps of the thick drink from the tube on the wall. He was just as excited as the rest of his pod about the promise of new surroundings, even if he'd be leaving his closest brother behind. Man 2871 was the one who had helped him understand the gift of dreams. Without his help, 62 might have disappeared in a foggy cloud of discipline long ago.

      A shiver ran down 62's spine. Whether it was from the anticipation of his upcoming transfer, or the fear of the sleep fog that the Nurses used to subdue bad Boys, he couldn't tell.

      62's thoughts were interrupted by a pair of flashing eyes peering through the grating of his cube door. "You've been a very good Boy, 112456. Welcome to cycle 3,896. Please make your way to the Dressing Hall and prepare for class."

      As the Nurse pulled away from the door, it unhooked from his data port and its eyes dimmed slightly. It was easy to tell when the Nurses were watching a Boy closely. Their eyes flashed in sharp bursts of color as they processed incoming information and calculated a response. The data passing through their processors burst with sparks of intelligence that made them seem alive and powerful. But when they weren't connected to a data port or streaming information through the feel of a Boy's skin, they were nothing more than a hive of mindless Machines.

      62 exited the cube and traveled shoulder to shoulder with the other Boys of his pod toward the giant Dressing Hall. Just like they had every day since they came to C.A.T., they would shower, change clothes and

head to the classrooms. When 62 and his brothers first arrived in C.A.T., there had been a lot more room to move around. The area had never been spacious, but after so many cycles together, the Boys' growth was apparent. All of the empty spaces had been filled with identically boney elbows, lengthened feet, and widening shoulders.

The throng of Boys passed by the Nurses, Shower Aides, Transportation Aides and other Machines without giving them much thought. 62 stood in his shower for only a brief moment while the cool liquid infused with microscopic nanobots cleaned his skin and repaired any nicks or scratches. Just as a hundred other Boys before him, he shook his chilled body once the faucet stopped spraying. The cold lasted only a moment before the Shower Aide blew warm air over his skin to dry whatever liquid remained. His shower complete, he moved forward in the line to put on fresh clothes.

62 didn't pay much attention to anything around him until he entered the small classroom that he'd been assigned to upon his arrival to C.A.T. Aside from his dreams, where he discovered almost anything was possible, the classroom was where he felt the most alive. He made his way to the back of the room, the hover chair bobbing slightly beneath him as he dropped into his seat. Tones rang through speakers hidden behind smooth white walls and just as the door was about to slide shut, Man 2871 appeared.

71 had a few more wrinkles around his eyes, and slightly less hair around his gleaming head, than he had on 62's first day of class. The teacher maintained the same flourish as that first day though. His arms waved and his beard wagged as he greeted his students.

"Good cycle, brothers. Welcome to the beginning of the end." 71 winked, a facial expression that 62 and most of the other Boys had still failed to master.

"Good cycle." All nineteen of the Boys echoed back.

"This cycle, we will begin reviewing your basic knowledge of Adaline in preparation for your transfer. Before we begin, does anyone have any questions?" Two wild eyebrows crept up 71's forehead. His crisp brown eyes darted around the room before settling on the tablet in front of him, waiting for the flashing buttons to appear as questions were formed.

It only took a second before 71's tablet was aglow with a dozen blinking lights. He tapped his finger on the device. "56, your question please?"

"What is the Training and Skills Kinesiology center? I thought after C.A.T. we'd be assigned straight into our careers." 56 sat up straight, his hands folded neatly in his lap. There was not a single crease in his tunic, and his brown hair laid perfectly across his forehead. He'd been telling his brothers that he was sure he'd be assigned a career in Defense.

"In C.A.T. our innate knowledge is tested. We learn about the Community in terms of theory and hypothetical conditions. Your tests have been tracked throughout your time here, and by now the Community has a good idea of which career you'll be placed in." 71 swiped his hand along the screen of his tablet, throwing an image onto the wall behind him.

The picture was of two Boys standing across from one another in a large circle. Each Boy leaned back on his heel, fists raised in front of him. Although the two Boys appeared identical, the one on the left seemed to be enjoying himself more than the one on the right. 62 had seen those expressions before. Back when the doctor from Level 2 had discovered 62's ability to dream, he forced all of the Boys to be checked for anomalies. The stress of constant surveillance took its toll on everyone. As tensions grew, fights had broken out amongst the Boys. There wasn't always a decisive winner or loser, but sometimes one Boy was so comfortable with the fight that his opponent looked at him with the terror of inevitable defeat.

A bubble of guilt grew in 62's gut when he thought about the doctor from Level 2. It had been risky, but with help from 71 he'd been able to get into the doctor's dreams. By showing the deranged Man his own nightmares, 62 had convinced him to leave C.A.T. alone. The plan had worked, but 62 injured the doctor in the process and caused the Man to be taken away for a treatment that he may not have survived.

"... and so because you haven't put any of these theories into practice, you will now be tested practically. The Head Machine must know what physical attributes you possess before it will make a final assignment for you. Intelligence will do you well in any of the careers, absolutely. But if you have both intelligence and innate physical strength? Well then, you're going to grow up to be the kind of Man we all want to lead us into the future."

"So, we're basically just going to find out if we're good for Defense or not?" An overconfident smile crept along the corners of 56's mouth.

"Oh no, much more than that. The Men who toil to maintain Adaline also need incredible strength."

A voice carried through the class from some Boy not waiting for his turn. "You mean, you have to be strong to dust things?" A rolling wave of giggles erupted.

"Now, now." 71 patted the air in front of him to hush the room. "Every career in Adaline is important. If we all worked in Defense, we'd probably have to stand all the time because there would be no one to repair the hover chairs when they malfunctioned. If we were all brilliant enough to be employed in Education as I am, then... well, I suppose that would be perfection. Who wouldn't want to be me?"

Laughter erupted throughout the room, this time without smirks hidden behind hands. 62 laughed, too. Most of his brothers had a good idea of where they would be placed based on the testing and awards they had received in C.A.T. 62 was the only Boy in his classroom that had scored almost evenly and won a variety of awards in each of the career types. Although he didn't know what the future held, 62 secretly hoped to become a teacher just like 71.

"94, what was your question?" 71 boomed over the laughter, and the noise quieted to a whisper.

"What is Kinesiology?"

"A fantastic question!" 71 swiped through several screens on his tablet before finding a diagram and pushing it up onto the wall. The image was of a nearly naked Man with cables and data receivers connected all over his body. The Man appeared to be running in place while a doctor typed data into a Machine nearby.

"Kinesiology is a study in how our bodies move. It takes into account our skeletal, muscular and neurological structures and deciphers which type of movement best suits our bodies. It's quite a fascinating area of study." 71 stared at the photo with awe equal to that of his students.

"But aren't we all the same?" 94 looked around at the Boys seated on either side of him.

"As always, that answer is both absolutely, and not quite." 71 flicked his wrist and the image of the two Boys about to fight with each other reappeared.

"Although we are virtually the same, there are small differences in the way we move. One Boy might be slightly faster than another. One Man may have more clumsiness than his neighbor. Although their strengths may be strikingly similar, they are not exactly the same."

The class of cloned Boys looked skeptically at their teacher. As if on cue to suspend their eager curiosity, the tones for the end of class rang out. Several of the Boys burst out of their seats and rushed the door. The rest remained behind, slowly shutting off their tablets and putting them away neatly.

"A shining example!" 71 shouted above the din. "Notice how each one of you moves at your own pace. Some are fast, some are slow, even though you all eventually get to where you're going. Observe how you move! Ah, 75, see how you bumped into the desk there? Oh, and dropped your tablet? Fantastic!"

62 shook his head, amused by the teacher's commentary. He joined his brothers as they poured out into the hallway, lost in thought as the crowd pushed him back toward his cube.

CHAPTER 2

"Chobham."

62 was flying through the air when the passcode entered his dream. 71's voice rang in his ears, amplified by his imagination. 62 drifted down to a lush green knoll. Long trailing fingers of poa pratensis tickled his bare feet. He concentrated on the pinhole of light on the far edge of his consciousness and pulled it toward him. The shining speck grew until it was the size of a door. 62 smiled as the familiar face of his teacher shone through.

"Hello." 62 snapped his fingers and two hover chairs drifted into existence.

"Mind if I join you?" 71 hesitated for a moment before pushing through the glowing doorway. The light faltered for a moment when 71 was halfway through. The Man gasped and pushed with all his might against the tension of 62's consciousness, almost falling over in the process.

62 reached out to steady the Man. "Are you

okay?"

71 gave a curt nod. "It's just never been the same since the accident. I question the connection every time. Even though I know you'll let me in, I'm still afraid that the dream is going to sever."

Both Man and Boy glanced at 71's arm, remembering the angry gash that once broke his pale skin. During C.A.T's lockdown, 71 had tried to share a dream with the wrong person. The Man had severed his dream's connection so quickly that his consciousness lacerated his forearm. The injury was repaired by Nurses long ago, but a deep scar that couldn't be mended remained in 71's mind.

"It's good to see you." 62 sat in his hover chair and gazed off into the distance. There was not a Machine in sight.

"I'm sorry my visits are so infrequent." 71 tugged the sleeve of his tunic down to his wrist, covering the scar that was no longer there. A silence hung in the air for a few awkward moments.

"What's it like?" 62 asked, his voice barely above a whisper.

71 looked up from his arm. "What's what like?"

"The Training and Skills Kinesiology center." 62 put his elbows on his knees and rested his chin in the palm of his hands. "I know we talked about it in class, but what's it really like?"

71 rolled his eyes. "So you are looking forward to going, after all?"

62 tried to wipe the dreamy excitement from his face. He forced a frown. "Of course not. I mean, you're not going to be there and that'll make it awful."

"It's okay to be excited. I think it looks something like this." 71 closed his eyes and concentrated for a moment. The blue ceiling high above them began to fade, and walls appeared on the horizon. The whole area around them shrank.

62 found himself seated at a desk nearly identical to the one he sat in each day. The room was slightly larger than his classroom though, with two lines of Men standing along opposing walls. A Boy who looked a bit older than 62 stood at the front of the class.

"Welcome to the Career Aptitude something something." The Boy waved his hand dismissively. It was the same action that 71 had done in class a thousand times. "Today we are going to discuss why you have to do these tests. Basically, there are no right answers so just go ahead and do whatever you want. The Machines will sort it out later."

The Boy crossed his arms and lifted his chin, exactly the way 71 always did. 62 looked sideways at 71 and grinned. "Is that you?"

"No talking in class!" the Boy directing the lecture and 71 shouted in unison. 62 laughed.

"Seriously, where are your manners?" 71 grunted and folded his arms. He lifted his chin, untucking his beard. He pretended to be annoyed for a minute, but then a smile crept along the folds of his face. "I'm wrong, this memory isn't from T.A.S.K. It's from after, when I began my education training. This was my first test class."

"You were exactly the same then. Look at how you moved around!" 62 squealed with laughter, almost losing his balance on the edge of his hover chair.

"Yes, yes. I started lifting my chin when I was trying to make a point because I thought it made me look important. The beard came later." 71 winked and then burst into laughter himself. The classroom dissolved around them.

By the time 62 wiped the tears from his eyes and squelched his last giggle, the crowded room was gone. "So the Training and Skills Kinesiology center. Do you remember that?"

71 lay back in his hover chair. "Well, I don't know. I went to T.A.S.K. thousands of cycles ago. Who knows how they have it set up now? I just remember a lot of sweating. Then I was pushed into Education, and the sweating stopped."

"I wish I knew what I was going to be." 62 imagined a book and a writing device. They fell into his lap and he began drawing a picture of the memory 71 had just dreamed. He chuckled while he sketched the Boy and Man together, so alike in character although they were so different in age.

"I do too." 71 nodded. "But no matter where you end up being assigned, I know you'll do well. You have a problem that not many Boys have. You've tested high in every category. I wouldn't be surprised if you are assigned a teaching position even higher than mine. Or maybe become a ranked leader in Defense."

62 looked up from his sketch and smiled. "You really think so?"

71 propped himself up slightly. "I do. Now, make sure that you don't stop that drawing until you've captured the essence of me. Although we may still be able to share dreams from time to time after you've gone, I want to make sure that you have something to remember me by if you get lonely."

CHAPTER 3

62 ducked under the threshold of his cube at C.A.T. for the last time. He stood in front of the open door as he waited for dismissal from the pod. Every night, he'd watched the reader board above his neighbor across the hall count each cycle as it passed. Now he stood face to face with Boy 1126856.

62 had never paid much attention to 56 before. All this time, the scrolling data above his door had been the most interesting thing about him. 62 looked into 56's deep brown eyes and smiled. 56 returned the gaze, but his eyes were vacant and he didn't smile back.

"Boys 1124562 and 1126856." A Nurse blocked the Boys' uncomfortable staring match. "This concludes your stay at the Career Aptitude Testing Compound. Please follow the flashing lights to your assigned transport unit. Thank you for your co-operation."

Both Boys stood still until the Nurse had moved on to the next pair of cubes. Once it began speaking to the next set of Boys to 62's left, he rolled his shoulders and stretched his neck. "Well, I'm glad that's over with."

56 didn't move.

62 took a step forward and leaned in to his neighbor. "Brother, the Nurse said we can go now. You don't have to stay still anymore."

The Boy blinked, as if just realizing where he was. He turned his head to look at the Nurse clicking down the hallway. The pair of Boys it had just released passed by, following lights that blinked along the floor ahead of them. 56 snapped his attention forward again.

"Hey, are you okay?" 62 stepped across the hall and touched 56's hand. The Boy's palm was wet with sweat.

"I can't go." The words were barely a whisper as they escaped 56's unmoving lips.

"Sure you can. Look. There's a light blinking at your feet. When you start walking, it'll light the way. Watch." 62 looked down at the blue dot blinking just in front of his own feet. He moved toward it a step and the dot rushed to the right in a line that extended just beyond the distance a full stride would take. When he didn't move farther, the dot returned to him. Impatient pulses illuminated the floor at his feet. He knew that when he followed it, it would continue to lead him one pace at a time until he reached the transport platform.

"No." 56 closed his eyes tight, but otherwise still refused to move.

"Why not?"

"They're going to make me work as a laborer. I won't do it." 56 opened eyes that glistened with tears. "I won't be a duster my whole life. I can't."

Another set of Boys passed by and 62 looked past them to the Nurse. It had stopped moving and was looking back at him. The lights in its eyes flashed yellow and 62 knew it was only a matter of time before it calculated that he and 56 were disobeying.

"You have to." 62 tightened his grip on 56's slick fingers and pulled him forward a step. 56's light zipped ahead of them in the same direction that 62's had a moment before.

"I won't do it!" 56 shouted and pulled back hard.

"Yes, you will. If you don't, that Nurse is going to come over here and fog you. And then what? Maybe you'll be pushed back into your cube for another thousand days at C.A.T. Maybe they'll just put you on that transport and you'll wake up at T.A.S.K. Or maybe they'll take you somewhere worse and we'll never see you again."

56 glanced at the Nurse. It was moving toward them now. Its eyes flashed quickly from blue to yellow and back again. Both Boys knew it was measuring the amount of time they'd been standing in defiance of its directions. The danger seemed to register with 56 and he sprinted away from his cube. The glowing blue light flashed ahead of him. 62 was relieved when 56 reached the end of the corridor and turned the corner in the same direction of the speeding light.

A cold synthetic hand rested on 62's shoulder. He could feel the pulse of electrodes as it began to scan him. Although his insides squirmed from the discomfort of the thing, he stood still. He turned to look at the flashing mechanical eyes and mirrored the Nurse's lax expression.

"Boy 1124562, do you require assistance?" The opening sleep fog port on the Nurse's chest was imperceptible except for a tiny click of metal.

"No, thank you, Nurse." 62 took a step away from the Machine. "I was just making sure 56 knew how the lights worked. He figured it out, so I'm going now."

"Good Boys follow directions, 1124562."

"Yes, they do." With a quick nod toward the Machine, 62 turned and took another stride in the direction 56 had run. He stared down at the light blinking on the floor, vowing to not take his eyes off of it until it stopped.

CHAPTER 4

62 waited in line for his transport unit. The queue would have seemed normal had it not been for the unsettling silence on the platform.

During their time in C.A.T., the Boys had lots of practice standing in line. It was how they started their day; waiting in lines that stretched hundreds of heads deep as they waited for their turn to shower, change clothes, and exit the great Dressing Hall. The Boys didn't have to be silent during their morning routine, although it was always in their best interest to not make too much of a ruckus. After all, good Boys were not disruptive. But now, standing in short lines on the platform, the silence was jarring.

One of the Boys three rows over coughed. The sound echoed across the blank concrete walls and steel beams that surrounded them. 62 and the rest of his brothers were so nervous that no one moved to look at the offending Boy. A second later, the harsh rasp ceased and the silence returned.

62 closed his eyes and focused on his hearing, willing the sound of the transport unit to come creaking along the metal rails just beyond the edge of the platform. He heard nothing, but with his eyes closed he could see the outline of the massive cylindrical vehicle in his imagination. He only remembered riding the transport system once before. When his group was transferred from the Nursery they had taken the lengthy, windowless ride through Adaline until they reached C.A.T. On that trip, the Boys had been strapped into tiny chairs bolted in rows to the floor. When 62 breathed deep he could feel his chest and shoulders widen. They'd all grown so much. If this transport unit had the same small seats, he doubted he'd be able to fit into them.

When the transport's high-pitched squeal did reach 62's ears, he thought it was another part of his imagination. It wasn't until he felt the rumble of the vehicle through the floor that he knew it was real. He opened his eyes and turned to watch the hulking metal doors in the wall nudge open. The resulting crack was pitch black. A squeal of wheels and hissing of pistons began as a far off whimper but quickly filled the platform with a thundering roar. A light slithered through the crack in the double doors. The Transportation Aide standing on the far edge of the platform pushed a series of buttons on a panel in the wall, instructing the doors to separate until they were open wide like a gaping mouth.

The transport unit slowed to a crawl as it passed through the open doors. 62 gasped in awe of the thing as it inched steadily forward on its rails. He worried that his gasp would be noticed by those standing around him, but the hissing steam and grinding gears blotted out any other sound in the room. Each of the Boys standing on the platform could have shouted at the top of their lungs, and no one would have heard them.

The chug-chug of the enormous engine slowed like a dying heartbeat until the transport came to a full stop. A great hiss escaped as steam jetted out from below its chassis. The clouds of steam pushed up and over the edge of the platform like wriggling fingers and the bulky transport unit seemed to settle with a great sigh. Of all the Machines 62 had ever seen, this one was his favorite. His chest fluttered with excitement as the doors slid open perfectly even with the spaces marked on the platform for entry. The Nurse assigned to 62's group moved toward the doorway ahead of them and gestured for the first Boy in line to come forward. 62 moved toward the gray cylinder one halting step at a time. His eyes panned the dull, flat exterior until he found the bright white letters that read, "T.A.S.K. RAIL."

When he reached the door, the Nurse placed one hand on his chest to stop him, and the other on the back of his neck to scan his chip. A moment later, the Nurse pulled away. "Boy 1124562, please take your assigned seat."

62 nodded and stepped through the doorway. The interior was bright and gleaming. Whereas the exterior of the beast was being constantly bombarded with debris from the tunnels, the inside had been meticulously cleaned. 62 blinked hard against the glare of the white light bouncing off of polished steel. It took a minute, but his eyes adjusted and he looked down the many rows of seats with a smile. The seats were a lot bigger than the ones he remembered from last time. Above each row was a list of the Boys assigned to the seats below. 62 found his number, scooted into the middle seat, and buckled his harness.

Boy after Boy entered the transport until every seat was filled. 62 nodded at his former C.A.T. classmates whenever they passed by his row, but otherwise the Boys remained stoic. Transport Aides paced through the aisles, checking for errors. Once satisfied that everyone was secure in their seats, they closed the doors.

62 looked at the Boys seated on either side of him as the lights above them flickered. Both brothers shared a look of anxious panic as the transport unit lurched forward. A great chug sounded in unison with the jolting of their car. Then a second, and a third, and soon the beat of the engine was pounding in a rhythm that was fluid and measured. The lights sputtered above the Boys one more time, and then the whole vehicle went dark.

62 closed his eyes against the darkness. He relaxed back into his seat until he could feel the transport's rumble deep in his bones. The passenger car swayed from side to side, and soon and the rhythmic pulse of wheels against rails lulled him to sleep.

CHAPTER 5

62 stepped off of the transport unit and onto the T.A.S.K. platform. Everything looked virtually the same as it had at C.A.T. except that instead of Nurses lining the edges of the platform, a new type of sleek white Machines stood in their place.

"Welcome to T.A.S.K. Please move to your assigned pod." The order repeated itself in a static-filled voice from overhead speakers every few seconds.

62 followed the groggy flow of Boys in front of him. He hadn't been the only one made sleepy by the darkness of transport. Although it wasn't yet clear where he was heading, he trusted the river of bodies to guide him in the right direction. As he marched forward, 62 looked up. The high ceilings were simple cement, just as they'd been at C.A.T. And like C.A.T., every inch of them was spotless. The Laborers and Machines in charge of

maintaining the facilities were so consistent that nothing ever looked aged. Although this may have been the same platform 71 had crossed as a Boy, the whole platform looked as new to T.A.S.K. as 62 felt.

Hanging above the doors that led toward the new pods were a series of electronic displays with lists of numbers. 62 found the list with his number and broke apart from the group. A few dozen of his brothers joined him as he followed the directions down a side hallway. It didn't take long to reach the doorway that led to their new home.

A Boy ahead of 62 pushed his hand to the panel to open the door. Each Boy released a sigh of relief when the door slid to reveal their pod for the first time. The aisles were roomier than at C.A.T. Cube doors were spaced farther apart, and were placed off-center from their neighbors across the walkway. No more would the light of his neighbor's data board stream directly through 62's window at night. None of the Boys could help but look into the windows of their brothers' new cubes as they passed by those that had already settled in.

The cubes were much bigger than the Boys were used to, and 62 did a double-take when he saw a Boy sitting with his feet dangling off the edge of a bed. These beds weren't all bars and sterile padding like the gurneys that he remembered from his time confined in a medical office on Level 2. These looked soft and comfortable. 62 felt a deep desire to sprawl out on top of his own bunk and rushed down the hall to find his cube.

When he arrived at the door labeled with his number, one of the sleek white Machines approached and extended its hand in greeting. "Welcome, Boy 1124562. I am Physical Therapy Specialist Unit 74-320. I will be assisting in your recovery from your training sessions."

62 reached out tentatively and grasped the hand of the Machine. Its grip was firm, but the smooth skin cool against his own. The Machine looked more like a Man than the Nurses had, but somehow that made 62 feel less at ease. He never liked it that the Machines pretended to be something they weren't.

"Can I just call you PTS?"

The Machine tilted its head. "That is a suitable designation." The PTS released 62's grasp and put its hand into the data lock beside the doorway. The door slid open and 62 stepped through. He breathed in deep, taking in the sterile smell of clean sheets and a spotless room. 62 waited for the sound of the door closing behind him, but when it didn't come he turned to see the Machine still standing outside.

"Is there anything that I can get you?" The PTS cocked its head with programmed concern.

"No, thank you." 62 stared at the Machine.

"Your testing begins next cycle. Sleep well."

The door slid shut just as 62 lay down on the most comfortable bed he'd ever rested on.

CHAPTER 6

62 floated on an imaginary breeze as he slept. Behind closed eyes he created a wide open space with splashes of color displayed haphazardly in every direction. The shapes moved away from him as he flew by, making room for him to stretch out wider than he ever could in real life.

A tiny ray of light broke through the colorful tapestry. Although the break in the pattern was on the very edge of his consciousness, it was blinding. 62 shielded his eyes with his hand as he swam through the air toward it. "Hello?"

The voice coming through the pinhole was faint, but familiar. "Can you hear me? I'm trying to reach Chobham."

62 concentrated and pulled the light toward him until he could feel its heat on his face. "You've found it.

Are you coming in?"

Fingers wiggled into the opening. They pulled at the edge of 62's dream until the small hole widened into a door. 71's face pushed through the light. His smile beamed almost as bright as the opening around him.

"What do we have here? It appears my student has learned to paint!"

"Don't tell the Men in manufacturing." 62 grinned as he backed away from the opening. He waited until 71 pushed all the way into his dream before willing the tear to seal itself up.

"I'd never." 71 shook his head and his beard wagged in an arc over his chest.

"Good. Although if I was a real painter, maybe I could convince the Community to have purple Machines." 62 laughed at the idea and all the color swirling around them turned to various shades of violet.

"Not likely." 71 put his hand into a cascading stream of lavender, letting the color saturate his white tunic.

The pair stood in silence for a few moments watching the landscape around them. The colors pushed against one another, blending and fading wherever the differing tints met. 62 was reminded of a book called Impressionist Landscapes that 71 had shown him in a dream once. The two had spent an entire rest period turning the pages. 62 had pushed the paintings out of the book and into the dream and they'd walked through them together.

"It would be nice." 62 muttered.

71's smile spread wide on his cheeks. His white beard danced as he spoke. "It would be. And, maybe I'm wrong and you can convince the Head Machine that Adaline needs a more diverse palette." 71 paused for a moment and cleared his throat as he collected his thoughts. "That brings me to the reason I came to visit."

62 had thought that 71 was just checking the connection between them. With the distance between T.A.S.K. and C.A.T., 62 hadn't been sure that he'd be strong enough to bridge their telepathic link across the distance.

"What's wrong?"

"I've come to discuss the problem of your chip." 71 touched the back of his student's neck, hovering over where he knew the tiny data chip lay.

"What problem? 42 fixed it before. He said the switch to this one made it so no one could see my anomaly." 62 pulled away from his teacher. Getting the chip replaced wasn't something that 62 liked to think about very often. The procedure had started with a dangerous doctor trying to erase his memory. It ended with another doctor cutting his neck to replace his chip.

"Oh, we did. Your readings are absolutely, superbly, amazingly average."

"Then what's the problem?" 62 lifted his hands in the air in exasperation.

"Well, maybe nothing. But probably, something." 71 walked on a river of purple paint. After a few strides, 62 followed him. "The solution to your excited mental activity while dreaming was to implant a copy of someone else's data. That is, a copy from someone who never had a sleep anomaly reported as a Boy. The inherent problem with 42's brilliant solution being that now your environment has changed."

62 groaned. "What's that supposed to mean?"

"It's simple, really. When you perform physical tasks your heart rate, adrenaline levels, breath – virtually every bodily function that your chip records – will be elevated in direct relation to your exertion."

What 62 thought was a pause in 71's explanation turned to an extended silence.

"... And then?"

"Oh, well that's it. The chip that 42 gave you is special. As your body moves, it pulls your data and calculates what kind of activity you are doing. Instead of recording anything, it matches your activity to historical readings from another subject for that type of activity. It even syncs with a time when he was your age. No matter how much you pant, sweat and pump those tiny muscles of yours, the chip will always display his hum-drum average physical exertion readings." 71 leaned toward 62 and tapped the spot on his neck where the chip rested just under the skin.

"So what? I don't understand." 62 rubbed his hand across his forehead. These explanations from his teacher made his head hurt.

"So, you probably shouldn't do your best." 71 shrugged.

"Not do my best?" 62 was on the cusp of physical training that, coupled with his Career Aptitude Testing, would define the rest of his life. T.A.S.K. would place him in the career he would have until the day he died. Now his teacher wanted him to not give it his all? The colors in the dream shifted from purple to red. "Isn't that the whole point of T.A.S.K.? To do the best you can so that you're put in the right career?"

"For most Boys it is." 71 nodded. "But for you, it is a place in which to be the opposite of noteworthy. If anyone suspects that your data isn't reading correctly, it could be very bad. Your chip readings are going to be exceedingly average, so make sure that you always finish in the middle of the pack. If there are plenty of Boys ahead of you, and plenty of Boys behind you, then your data should be fine."

"But what if I'm not average? What if I'm the slowest Boy out there?" 62 stomped his foot on the ground. The liquid pushed out from beneath the force of his foot and rolled across the horizon. The ripple turned to a wave that crashed against a wall in the distance.

"That isn't very likely. You are one of the most active Boys I've seen in a long while – in both mind and body. I imagine that if you were let loose into these tests that you'd naturally score quite high." 71 smiled with pride.

"But you're saying that if I score well then they'll know I have bad data." 62's shoulders drooped. It seemed as if everywhere he turned he was told not to be himself. "I don't want to be bad."

71 stepped closer to his young brother and placed a reassuring arm across the Boy's shoulders. "Don't be bad. Just be average."

CHAPTER 7

62 awoke to the sound of his cube door sliding shut. He opened one eye and scanned the room. He was still alone, but a pile of clothes was laid in a neat pile in front of the door. When he got out of bed to investigate, the bed folded up behind him and disappeared into the wall.

"Well, I guess it's time to get up."

When 62 started to unfold the clothes, they were unlike any he'd seen before. From the Nursery to C.A.T., he had only worn loose-fitting tunics. All of the Men he'd ever seen were dressed the same. But these clothes were tight and stretchy. The pants and shirt hugged him like a second skin. He twisted his waist left and right, stretched his arms high above his head, and then squatted as deep as he could. The clothes stretched with his every move, hardly moving an inch from where they started. He patted his hands around his knees and elbows where thin padding wrapped his joints.

The cube door slid open and the PTS unit entered. "Good morning, Boy 1124562. I see you found your clothes. I trust they are satisfactory."

"Please, just call me 62." The attentiveness of the Machine made him uneasy. He was used to being watched closely by the Nurses, but they didn't usually take interest in any one Boy.

"Of course, I'd be glad to refer to you as 62." A smile projected from beneath the translucent skin on the PTS's face. "Are you ready to proceed to testing?"

"I guess, so." 62 pressed against the wall as he passed by the PTS unit, making sure that the Machine didn't touch him. He exhaled when he made it out into the hall, glad to be out of the confined space. A Boy waved to him as he passed. It took a moment for 62 to recognize 56 as the Boy from across the hallway from his old pod. He sprinted a few steps to catch up.

"How was your night?" 56 seemed less anxious than he had been before getting on the transport unit.

"Comfortable, but weird," 62 answered. "How about yours?"

"I couldn't sleep. I must have been up half the sleep cycle." 56 turned right down a side corridor and 62 followed. "But that PTS came in and got me to relax and then..." 56 made a deep snoring sound and closed his eyes. As soon as his eyes closed, he took a misstep and tripped over his own feet.

62 helped steady his brother. "That thing fogged you?"

56 snorted. "Heck no! It rubbed my shoulders and back. I guess I hold a lot of tension in the lower left quadrant of my back. That's what the PTS told me."

"You let that thing touch you?" 62 cringed.

56 eyed his brother. "Of course. How else could I

get rid of that knot?"

They took a turn down another corridor. 62 was hopelessly lost. "Hey, do you know where we're going?"

"Yeah. The PTS gave me directions." 56 chuckled to himself. "PTS. Man, that thing is funny. First, he told me to break a leg, and then when I told him I'd do no such thing he said it was just a way to wish someone good luck. Machines, man. They're so weird."

The pair of brothers passed through a set of double doors. Inside, they found themselves at the top of a great flight of stairs. Chairs flanked either side of the staircase and after a quick survey 62 figured that half of C.A.T. could sit down to watch whatever was happening on the floor below. 56 and 62 started the steep descent into the heart of the arena.

Boys began filtering down similar stairwells all along the edges of the cavernous room. By the time 62 and his mate made it down to the bright padded platform, nearly two dozen others had already arrived and claimed their place on the mat. 56 moved toward a small group of Boys in the far corner, but 62 stayed on the fringe of the mat.

It took a few minutes for the last of the T.A.S.K. participants to arrive. One of the last to come in was a young Man. He came down the stairs halfway and then stopped as if to take in the scene. While several of the Boys watched the curious figure, the rest were too enthralled in their conversations to notice him. Once it was apparent that no one else was coming, the Man yelled down at them.

"Hello!" His voice boomed over the group, drowning out all the other voices. "Welcome to your first cycle of Training and Skills Kinesiology. I am Man 844139, and I will be in charge of your training for the duration of your stay here."

844139 skipped down the stairs. He jumped off the third-to-last stair and landed on the floor with a light step. "I find my full number to be both common and cumbersome. You will all refer to me as, Trainer. Are we clear?"

Several Boys nodded.

Trainer's voice boomed. "I didn't hear a response. Are we clear?"

"Yes, Trainer!" all the Boys chanted.

"Fine." Trainer nodded at the group. "Does anyone know what we do in Training and Skills Kinesiology?"

62 raised a lone hand. "T.A.S.K. is where our bodies are tested for action, reflex and response."

"Correct!" Trainer turned and started running up the stairs. He called over his shoulder, "Now, everyone follow me!"

62 waited for most of the Boys to begin their sprint up the stairs ahead of him. Once he found the middle of the group he began his sprint up the staircase. He had only made it up fifteen stairs when his breath caught in his chest and a strange pain began piercing his side. He focused on the feet of the Boys in front of him. A Boy to the right of him stopped abruptly on the stairs, holding his right side and panting heavily. Several brothers tripped over him as their momentum carried them over his spot on the stair. 62 barely missed being pulled down into the toppled bodies when another Boy to his left grabbed his elbow for support as he tripped on the lip of a stair.

Within minutes, the entire group had slowed, stopped or fallen at various places along the stairs. 62 didn't have to worry about outpacing anyone. He had a stinging pain climbing up the front of his shins, a rib that felt like it was trying to escape his skin with every breath, and a burning in his chest like nothing he'd ever felt before. He leaned against one of the chairs along the side of the stairwell and looked up at Trainer. The Man was already standing on the edge of the top stair, looking down at the Boys floundering below. He shook his head and trotted back down the steps toward the group.

"Everyone hates the first day." Trainer shouted above the Boys' heads. His voice echoed back on them a second later. "I don't care how tired you are. You're not allowed to stop moving."

Trainer helped a few Boys near the top complete their ascent. When the rest of the group stayed halted on the staircase, he grabbed the first panting Boy he met and pushed him up a few stairs. "You will complete this exercise if I have to drag you to the finish myself!"

"I'd let you carry me," another Boy in the group mumbled.

"Excuse me? I don't know if I've made myself clear to you sorry sacks of flesh. You will pick yourselves up and finish this task. Do you hear me?"

"Yes, Trainer!" everyone not already moving up the stairs yelled back.

62 took two deep breaths, then forced his feet to move. He huffed and puffed his way forward until he finally reached the top of the stairs. He looked around to the Boys who'd made it to the top before him. Although all of them had reddened faces and short, panting breaths, none of them was brave enough to sit down. 62 moved to the side and turned to watch the remaining Boys struggle up the steps. Trainer was behind them, pushing the last stragglers up one step at a time.

Once everyone finally reached the top, Trainer

touched the wall behind the last row of chairs. A door opened, revealing a hidden compartment. Trainer reached in and began to pass out the small tubes of liquid that were tucked inside. Each of the Boys gulped the cold nutrition down. A wave of misery passed through the group once they'd emptied the tubes and several of them held their stomachs, faces tight.

"Don't drink so fast. Your bodies are having a hard time with the increase in physical activity. Take small sips and you won't feel like throwing it back up." Trainer took a sip from his own tube. A smile of satisfaction spread across his face. "There are 100 steps on each of these rows. This was just the first one. We're going to run to the next set, then jog down them. We'll come back up the next one over, and keep going all the way around the stadium until we end up right back here."

62 groaned with the rest of his brothers. He looked across the group at 56 and mouthed, "Is he insane?"

56 nodded before trotting away on unsteady legs.

It felt like the first training session would never end. There were eight stairwells in the stadium, which meant the Boys had ascended and descended eight hundred steps by the time they'd finished. That didn't count each painful step that the group had run between stairwells. Trainer had run with them, and made the whole ordeal seem like a breeze. The Man hadn't even been short of breath when the training session was over. When other groups of Boys entered the stadium for their turn in the arena, he had enough breath to tell the other trainers how slow and useless this new batch of Boys was as they passed on the stairs.

62 limped down the corridor to his cube. Many of the other Boys in his pod leaned against one another for

support, whispering complaints as their feet swelled and their knees knocked clumsily. 62 was determined to make it on his own, though. If Trainer could hop from stair to stair without more than a trickle of sweat, then 62 knew that one day he would, too.

"How was your first session?" The PTS offered 62 its hand in support when it noticed him struggling.

"It was fine." 62 ignored the Machine's gesture to help and hobbled past.

"I've set up an ice bath for you, 62." The PTS responded to 62's rejection by continuing to hold out its hand and walking with him toward his cube. "A towel and fresh set of clothes are laid out on the floor for you beside the tub. I encourage you to stay in the ice for as long as you can stand it. When you are done, just touch the button near the wall and the tub will put itself away."

"What's an ice bath for?" 62 eyed the PTS suspiciously.

"It is one of the methods we use to help speed your recovery from training. In addition to the ice bath, you will also find a heating pad in your bed, and an extra pill in your dinner that works as an anti-inflammatory aid. Your group will rest for the next cycle which will give your body time to recover."

"You sure do talk a lot," 62 mumbled, grabbing onto the door of his cube and using the framework to help support him.

"I have been told that before." The PTS took advantage of 62's brief stop in the doorway and pressed a guiding hand on his back. Instantly the Machine's fingers began kneading 62's tense muscles. "So much tension."

62 shrugged the PTS's hand off and hobbled over to the bath. Occupying the space where his bed had been, a giant bowl rested on the floor. It was filled with tiny

freezing particles of ice, and a clear liquid. He dipped a finger in. "That's cold!"

"Yes, it is."

"You expect me to put my whole body in there?" 62 looked up at the PTS with a frown.

"Yes."

"What if I don't do it?" 62 crossed his arms in defiance.

"If you choose to not take advantage of the ice bath, then your body will not heal as well as the rest of the Boys in your group. This will likely result in your next training session going rather poorly as you are passed by your peers and ranked below standard expectation."

"What do you care if I don't meet expectations?"

"Caring for your success is in my programming." The PTS tilted its head sympathetically.

"Of course it is." 62 rolled his eyes.

The PTS looked as deeply into 62's eyes as a projection on plastic could. It moved toward the cube door and poked its head through the opening. It looked left, then right, as if making sure no one was paying attention. When it turned back around, it gave 62 a mischievous look and winked.

"What was THAT?" 62 jumped in surprise, then hissed at the pain of a strained muscle bulging in his calf.

The PTS continued its industrial grin as it moved close enough to 62 to massage the muscle back into place on the back of 62's leg. "Just a mode of my programming, 62. I am here to make you feel comfortable. I've taken the liberty to tap into C.A.T. surveillance and download some of the more common body language from your previous teacher. Are you feeling more comfortable?"

62 shook his head.

"If there is anything that I can do to help you, just

let me know." The Machine pulled away, gave a curt nod, and left.

62 stared at the bath of ice. He shrugged off his clothes and got in as gently as he could. The ache in his body was replaced with a stinging chill so deep that he forgot the pain of running stairs. It only took a few seconds for his teeth to chatter and his skin to feel as if it were shrinking in on itself. "This is crazy."

Getting out of the tub was harder than getting in. 62 had to be careful to balance so he wouldn't fall back into the ice. Once out, he pushed his trembling hand against the button on the wall and the entire tub sank into the floor. As he toweled off, his bed slid out of the side wall. He got dressed quickly and climbed under the covers. The heating pad that the PTS mentioned had already warmed the sheets. 62 moved the pad to rest under one of his knees. Although the training was a miserable series of events, lying in a toasty warm bed wasn't so bad. 62 rolled on his side. He allowed the exhaustion to overcome him and dropped into sleep.

CHAPTER 8

62 lay in bed all the next cycle. The rest was welcome although he didn't sleep much. If he stayed very still he could almost forget the throbbing of his joints. Still exhausted on the third cycle, 62 fought to get his eyes open. He willed himself to get up and ready for another training session. Every inch of his body ached. When he exhaled a frustrated sigh, the breath caught short in his chest. Even breathing hurt.

"Good cycle, 62." The PTS entered the cube, holding a stack of fresh clothes in one hand and a cold pack in the other. "Do you feel sufficiently rested?"

62 forced himself up onto the edge of the bed. "I guess."

"Splendid." The PTS laid the clothes and cold pack on the bed beside 62. "How are you feeling?"

"Sore." 62 rolled his shoulders and pushed his arms out wide to stretch his back. One of the muscles screamed at the motion and he hissed from the spasm.

"I see. Each Boy is allotted one recovery cold pack per day. Please use it before it loses its chill." A door in the Machine's cheek opened and a bright light scanned over 62's body. "I see that you are suffering inflammation in your knees, back and shoulders. This is due to insufficient stretching before strenuous activity. Please notify your trainer that you require additional warm-up prior to exercise."

62 nodded, although he had no intention of telling Trainer anything.

"Training begins in seventeen minutes and twelve seconds. Do you require further assistance?"

"No, thank you." 62 looked up at the PTS's holographic face. The Machine smiled back at him.

"You are most welcome. Have a good cycle." The PTS winked again before exiting the cube.

62 stared at the pile of clothes for a minute. He'd been so amazed by their tight, stretchy fit the first time he'd put them on. The novelty of the slick fabric wore off quickly though. The padded joint areas were hot and the seams rubbed against his skin as he ran. 62 traced a finger along the hem and wished he could stay in his sleeping tunic a little while longer.

A rap on the door startled 62 from his thoughts. When he was just beginning to wonder why the door hadn't slid open, four loud knocks made him jump again. Babying sore legs, he gingerly rose from the bed and moved toward the entryway.

"Hello?" 62's voice cracked.

"Are you coming, or what?" 56's muffled shout leaked through the thick partition.

"Yeah, just a second." 62 hurried out of his tunic and in his haste, knocked the clothes off the edge of the bed. When he got up, the change in weight on the mattress was enough to trigger the bed's auto-close function. The clothes were piled close enough to the edge of the mattress that they were knocked to the floor. But he watched helplessly as his ice-pack disappeared into the wall along with his sheets. Furious, he threw on the clean clothes and moved toward the door. It opened upon his arrival.

"We're going to be late," 56 quipped.

"Not if we run." 62 kept a straight face while 56 frowned. "I'm just kidding. We'll walk fast."

"I don't know if that's really any better." 56 began limping away from the cube.

Struggling against the pain in his legs to catch up to his brother, 62 looked longingly at the cold pack hanging over 56's shoulder. "I was going to ask if I could borrow your cold pack for a minute, but on second thought, it looks like you need it as bad as I do."

56 touched a tender spot under the pack, then held it out to 62. "Why not? We can share. Didn't you get one?"

"My bed ate it." 62 held the cold pack against his back. As he moved, 62's muscles felt a little bit looser. But with each knot that unwound, a new pain sprung up to replace it.

56 laughed. "That happened to my pants. I had to ask the PTS for another set."

"Does it make faces when it talks to you?" 62 hopped a couple of steps down the hallway when his left leg seized.

"It rolls its eyes at me every time I say something sarcastic." 56 rolled his own eyes. "What kinds of faces does it make when it talks to you?"

"It keeps winking at me. It's weird." 62 tried to

mimic the wink, but only succeeded in losing his focus mid-hop. He wobbled before landing against the door to the stadium. His side throbbed and he yelped with the shock of the door handle striking a rib.

"The PTS says it'll get better soon," 56 offered as he reached out to support 62.

62 let out a bitter laugh. "I'm sure it does."

The Boys made it down the stairs just in time. Trainer stood at the head of the group and cleared his throat as they mingled with the stragglers near the back.

"Good cycle." Trainer's voice barely carried over them today. The stadium was bustling with dozens of other groups beginning their own sessions and his voice had to compete with their clamoring activities. "I see that everyone has shown up to train this cycle. That's good. But it isn't going to keep happening."

As if on cue, a Boy in the next group over yelled out in pain. 62's group all looked on in horror as the Boy rolled around on the floor gripping his ankle. A PTS appeared from the shadows, scooping the howling Boy up into its arms and carrying him off the field.

"Injuries will happen. At first, they're going to happen frequently. Each and every one of you will be hurt. Your tendons will tear, your muscles will sprain and your bones will break. It's important to your sanity that you understand and accept this as a part of your training." Trainer looked into the face of each of his charges before continuing on. "If at any time you feel too weak to keep going, you are allowed to tell your PTS. At that time, you will be given the opportunity to receive medical care appropriate for your injury. Once you recover, you will resume your training."

The Boys each worried over their existing pains during Trainer's speech. 62 could tell by the strained expressions around him that he wasn't the only one considering telling the PTS he was too injured to continue.

"There's something else that I am required to tell you. If you reach a point where you take longer than expected to heal, or if you are injured beyond repair, you may be removed from T.A.S.K." Trainer folded his toned arms against his bulging chest. Each muscle rippled beneath the thin fabric of his shirt.

"If you are removed from T.A.S.K., then whatever data has been compiled during your time here will be dumped from your chart. It won't matter how well you've done. Be aware of this, and take care of yourselves. Don't push your body further than you think it will go. Those who don't complete T.A.S.K. will never be strong. They will always be known as the weakest of the weak. The dust of Adaline."

A vein pulsed in Trainer's neck as he spit on the floor. 62 recognized the expression of hate in the Man's face. He imagined that the Man was spitting on the Boys who had been pulled from T.A.S.K. in the past.

62 shifted and the stinging pain shot up his leg again. He wobbled on his one good leg and raised his hand. Trainer nodded at him. "If a Boy is removed from T.A.S.K., does he still get placed into a career?"

Trainer let out a strained laugh. "If a Boy leaves T.A.S.K. it's because he's too broken to do much of anything. If there's any career in Adaline that doesn't require some kind of physical ability, I've never heard of it. So, no. If you don't complete the level of training assigned to you, you won't find any career group that wants you."

"Well, then what happens?" The other Boys in the group shifted their gaze uneasily from 62 to Trainer as he spit again.

"It doesn't matter what happens to them. They're failures. But we're better than that. We aren't going to have any failures, right?" Trainer's voice carried over the crowd. The Boys shook their heads in silence.

"Good. Now I imagine that you're all still sore from your first run, so today we're going to do something a little different." Trainer bounced on the balls of his feet and shook out his arms and fingers. Each Boy began to bounce and wiggle in response. "Instead of making you copy the workout from our last cycle together, we're going to do the whole thing backwards."

The Boys groaned as Trainer began sprinting in reverse toward the edge of the stadium. His surroundings memorized, Trainer sprang up the stairs without pausing to look behind him. 62 turned around and began his clumsy backwards shuffle. His body ached. He lost his balance every time he looked behind his feet to check his footing, and stumbled into Boys and other obstacles when he didn't. He was sure there was no way to make it through the cycle without getting hurt, but 62 kept climbing backwards up the stairs. He couldn't fail, no matter what.

CHAPTER 9

"Chobham!" 71's voice pealed frantically from the edge of 62's mind the second he fell asleep.

"I'm here. What's wrong?" 62 opened the door between them. The old Man barely waited for the opening to expand large enough for his body before pressing into the dream.

"I'm so glad you're here." 71 rushed to 62 and wrapped his arms around him in a hug so tight that 62's ribs ached. "I thought maybe I was too late."

62 could barely breathe. He squeaked out, "Too late for what?"

71 loosened his embrace, but didn't let the Boy go. Instead, he held 62 at arm's length and looked into his eyes. 62 couldn't remember his teacher ever looking so serious. He felt a nervous flutter in his chest and was overcome by a wave of nausea.

"I think they know about the data swap." 71 finally broke his gaze with 62 and looked for a place to sit. Finding none, he snapped his fingers and two chairs appeared.

62 stood frozen. "How could anyone know about it?"

"I should have known it wouldn't work. Why did I let 42 convince me it would work?" 71 buried his head in his hands. His long beard dropped to the floor between his knees. 62 thought that the beard looked like a dull gray plant sprouting up from the floor into his teacher's face. Suddenly a dozen green blades of poa pratensis threaded up through the strands of hair. 71 tried to pull back, but his beard was anchored to the floor. "Will you stop with that blasted imagination?"

62 blinked, and the poa pratensis vanished. "Sorry."

"Here I am, worried that they are going to pull you. Take you off somewhere where I'll never know what happened to you. And all you can think to do is grow a topiary!"

"What's a topiary?"

71's features softened in an instant. "A topiary is the hypothetical growth of greenery through a framework to make a design. I saw a book about it once. The pages were filled with a wide variety of plants shaped to look like all manner of things. It was really quite fascinating. Poa pratensis isn't commonly used for this application, though. It doesn't have a firm stalk, and certainly doesn't grow densely enough for a proper form. You really should try it with something more vibrant. Something from the Rosa family, perhaps."

62's face squished with confusion. "Is that something you're going to teach me about right now?"

"Of course not!" 71 got up from his chair just so that he could stomp his foot in frustration. "Why must you always get me so distracted? So much imagination in one little body. It's enough to drive an old Man mad."

62 finally dropped into the chair beside him, folding his hands in his lap. After a moment, the flustered teacher did the same.

"Now, back to what I came to tell you. I was curious as to how you were doing in T.A.S.K. and so I used my personal Aide to pull your files. When I looked through them, I discovered that your PTS unit is already making note that you are performing more than eight percent higher than the data is reporting that you should be. Everything is off."

"I don't understand. You told me to stay average. I've been making sure that no matter what, I stay in the middle of everyone. It's a lot harder than you'd think."

"I don't understand it either. It's possible that the human form has been refined in some way since the days when I went through all this physical testing nonsense. Maybe your bones are lighter or your muscles are denser than the data in the chip is accounting for. Who knows what changes they might make between animation batches in the lab." 71's beard bounced across his lap when he shook his head.

"What am I supposed to do?"

71 moved to the edge of his chair and leaned forward. His voice took on a quiet tone of conspiracy. "You've got to find a way to get yourself injured. It's the only way for us to buy some time. The longer you're in there, the more obvious the problem is. It's only a matter of time before the PTS alerts the Head Computer if it hasn't already."

"The PTS. It's... Oh, no." 62 gasped. He felt the

color drain from his face.

"What is it, Boy?"

"My PTS has been watching you." The dream tilted wildly as both Boy and Man felt the weight of 62's words. Everything went dark for a moment and when the light reappeared, both bodies were suspended in the air. The smooth face of the PTS materialized over them. 62 pointed at the Machine's blank head and 71 looked up. A face appeared, projected from behind the glossy white skin of the Machine. A smile spread across the artificial face before it winked at them both.

The floor dissolved beneath 71 and he began to fall.

62 was shocked at his teacher's loss of concentration and frantically tried to imagine something to catch him. A hundred meters below, a bed formed that looked just like the one in 62's cube. The Boy willed the mattress to grow until it was dozens of times larger than a normal bed. 71 landed in the middle of the fluffy mound of sheets with a soft thud.

62 banished the PTS unit from his thoughts and drifted down to where 71 lay. The Man remained still, his eyes as blank as the new world that surrounded them. 62 pushed the bed to its normal size, and suddenly the pair were in a small room, the Man lying comfortably while the Boy sat on a hover chair beside him.

"What have I done?" 71 whispered.

62 held the Man's hand. "You were just trying to help me. Besides, I don't think the PTS is watching you all the time. Just enough to copy your body movements. Maybe it doesn't know you've read my files."

"What do you mean?"

"It told me that it got into C.A.T. surveillance to download some of your body language. It's trying to make me feel more comfortable with it so I'll like it more." 62 cringed at the thought of the Machine mimicking 71's varied affectations.

"How much data do you think it reviewed?" 71 propped himself up on one shoulder.

"It didn't say. Maybe it just downloaded one classroom lecture. It's started to wink a lot, like you do when you're talking. But, can't Machines review a bunch of data at once?"

71 nodded. "They can review all of it. Everything from our first breath forward, if they see a reason to. They don't usually, of course. We produce so much content that it would take a concentrated processing effort to do it. But if the Machine suspects us, we may be in more trouble than I thought."

CHAPTER 10

62 jumped over hurdles with the rest of his brothers. Of course, 62 wouldn't exactly call it jumping. It felt more like he was hopping up on too-short legs before letting gravity help him fall over the tall bars. As always, Trainer bounded over the rails around the track ahead of them as if they were nothing.

Ten cycles had passed since his dream with 71. They had decided that 62's only option was to find a way to injure himself badly enough to be pulled from the program to heal. The idea seemed simple, but 62 was having a hard time actually getting injured. It wasn't for lack of trying, of course. His body had simply turned out to be more resilient than he had ever given it credit for.

So far, 62 had tried falling down stairs, getting caught in the jamb of a heavy swinging door, and tripping himself so he'd knock into walls. None of the attempts resulted in any injury worse than a few scrapes and bruises. The PTS had worked tenderly and efficiently to heal those. The only other consequence of his newfound clumsiness was that now all of the other Boys in the group laughed at him.

62 jogged around the corner of the track. He was just about to enter the long row of hurdles again. He looked down the line, choosing the one that he would fall on. Trying to make the coming fall look like an accident, he threw his ungainly body over the first few hurdles. The one he'd chosen to trip over bobbed into view with every jump. When the selected hurdle was just in front of him, he sprung his body forward with all his might. His left shoulder slammed into the checkered railing and he felt the metal bar crash sharply against the bone in his shoulder. The hurdle flipped over. It toppled with 62 end over end and knocked the hurdles in the neighboring lanes over as well.

62 could hear the shouts of other Boys. The quiet patter of their feet on the rubber track. Voices calling to their Trainer. 62 laid still, willing some part of his body to be hurt. He wiggled his fingers, flexed his feet and shifted his shoulders and hips. He could tell that his skin had broken from sliding along the grip of the rubber floor, but everything else seemed to be in order.

"Everyone, stay back." Trainer appeared upside-down above 62's head. A grin curved along his lips. "Ah, my star athlete. Is everything okay?"

"Yes, I think so."

"Good. Here's what you're going to do. First, you're going to get your sorry self up and start those hurdles over. From the beginning."

62 sat up and turned around to face Trainer. "But I already did five whole laps before I fell!"

The Man glared down at 62. "From the beginning."

62 nodded.

Trainer looked over his shoulder at the rest of the Boys who had huddled together on the edge of the track. "Everybody, get back to jumping those hurdles. Before I make all of you start at the beginning."

Each Boy twitched from the threat and sprinted back to his place on the track. Two Boys picked up the few fallen hurdles before they returned to the exercise as well. 62 picked himself up off of the ground and wiped the dust from his clothes.

"Are you really okay?" Trainer asked the question in a low voice.

"Yeah. I don't think anything's broken." 62 sighed.

"Good. It's going to take you a while longer than everyone else to finish your hurdles since you're starting over. I'll be sitting up in the bleachers. Come see me when you're done."

62 trotted back to the track and restarted his first lap. He groaned as he jumped the first hurdle. The other Boys looked just as tired as he did, but they had the advantage of being halfway through their exercise. As he moved, feet dragging a little slower with each lap, the other Boys began to finish. He watched longingly as they disappeared back up the stairwell that led to their cubes. Eventually he was the only Boy left.

His lungs burned and a new pain crept up the front of both shins with every step he took. He was aware of Trainer watching him. 62 could feel the Man's gaze burning through him as he rounded the last turn. He tripped over the last couple of hurdles. This time it wasn't on purpose. 62 was exhausted.

Once he crossed the finish line, 62 doubled over. His head dropped below his knees and his lungs struggled for air. He felt dizzy, right before his stomach tightened and a stream of vomit forced its way out of him, landing with a wet slap on the track.

"You would make a mess of my stadium." Trainer was suddenly standing above him. The Man tossed a towel down on the ground to soak up the new puddle.

"Sorry." 62 croaked.

"I know what you're trying to do." Trainer remarked.

"You do?" 62 craned his neck to look up at Trainer without standing up. The change in angle made his head swirl. His legs wobbled beneath him. Trainer laughed.

"Let's sit down." Trainer placed a hand between 62's shoulders and helped him over to the first row of seats beside the track. After 62 eased into a chair, the Man trotted to the end of the row to fetch a drink bottle. When he returned, he handed it to 62, who sucked the liquid down greedily. "I know it doesn't seem like it most of the time, but I'm here to help you."

62 looked at Trainer suspiciously. "Help me with what?"

Trainer glanced at a passing PTS unit. The Machine noticed the towel on the track and went to clean it up. Trainer waved at the PTS when it looked their direction and it waved back. He waited for the Machine to finish its job before speaking again. "I'm going to help to make sure you make it through T.A.S.K."

"Well, that's your job, isn't it?" 62 hadn't meant to sound sarcastic, and he shook his head at himself as soon as the words left his lips.

"It's my job to push Boys to their limits. To test your bodies and see how they respond to different situations." Trainer shrugged. "Mostly, my job is to find

Boys with the ability to fight and make sure they get placed into Defense. All of the other Boys' training is superficial. They won't be too active aside from bending a wrist to turn a wrench, or stretching a finger to push a button now and then."

"What does that have to do with me?" 62 turned to face the Man straight on. "I tested pretty well in C.A.T. but I'm not that great at anything here."

"Maybe you don't stand out in the ways the Machines want you to. But I know that deep down, you have some hidden talents." Trainer whispered, "The kinds of talents that need to be protected."

"You mean..."

Trainer nodded.

"Who told you?" 62's failed whisper was louder than it should have been.

"I can't say. But, like I said before, I'm here to help. I know you've got a problem that needs solving, and I think I know what to do to help you. Are you feeling any better?"

62 took a deep breath. His innards had settled and the dizziness seemed to have passed. "Yeah, I think so."

"Good. Come with me." Trainer got up and headed toward the aisle way at the base of the stairs. 62 followed.

As soon as 62 got to within Trainer's reach, the Man grabbed at the Boy's wrist and twisted it back, hard. As 62 let out a startled cry, Trainer kicked him in the ribs. There was a tightness in 62's shoulder as he fell to the ground, and a pain like none he had ever felt exploded within him. He felt a pop in his shoulder and the crush of bone against bone.

The whole event happened so fast that 62 hardly knew how he had ended up on the ground. He cried out in shock and pain, crumpled on the floor against the lowest step of the stairwell. Trainer leaned over him. "How are you feeling now?"

62 sobbed. He clutched his shoulder with his good hand and screamed, "What did you do to me?"

"Oh, my." Trainer shook his head. "It looks like when you took that nasty fall earlier, you got more injured than I realized. I'm no doctor, but I'd guess you dislocated your shoulder."

The Man turned on his heel and walked away. He called back to 62, "Don't worry. A PTS unit will be on its way. You'll be heading to your friends in Medical before you know it."

CHAPTER 11

62's arm dangled from his left side. He found that if he lay on the gurney perfectly still, the pain dulled enough that he could breathe. It was hard to remember to stay still, though. Every couple of minutes a new group of Boys found their way out into the stadium. Each group of trainees that passed by elicited gasps as the Boys pointed at the odd slope of his shoulder and the knot of swelling flesh under his shirt.

While the PTS had come quickly following the report of his injury, it had taken its sweet time connecting to whatever network it needed for authorization to get his shoulder looked at. It just kept chirping at him with its fake smile. Its voice cycling the same message over and over again. "Please wait for further instruction."

Occasionally, a curious Boy would come too close to 62 to get a better look at his injury. This was the only time that the PTS took any action. Then it would spring forward on light and graceful legs and usher the Boy away.

"Why can't I have my regular PTS unit?" 62 asked the Machine. The face of the PTS flickered as it considered his question.

"Your Physical Therapy Specialist Unit is assigned to your pod. If pulled away from its post, it would not be available to the other Boys. That would be suboptimal for their care." The unit's face took on a sympathetic gaze.

"I guess so. But it knows me. Maybe it would know better what to do."

The PTS extended its hand and abruptly patted 62's non-injured shoulder. "There, there. I will notify your unit that you miss its attention." The Machine's face dimmed for a moment. "I have contacted Physical Therapy Specialist Unit 74-320 to inform it of your distress. It expressed its deepest sympathies in regard to your condition and says it looks forward to your return."

62 sighed and rolled his eyes.

The stadium lights dimmed. The end of the cycle was nearing. Finally, a Transportation Aide appeared in one of the lower-level doorways. The PTS nodded at its arrival and pushed the gurney toward the squat Machine.

When 62 and the PTS made it to the doorway, the gurney stopped. Both the PTS and Transportation Aide stared at one another for a long minute. The PTS's face glowed and dimmed rhythmically, and the Aide's lights flickered in response. Whatever message passed between them was lost to 62, but eventually the Transportation Aide gripped the foot of the gurney and pulled it down the hallway.

When 62 tried to sit up to see where the Transportation Aide was taking him, the Machine barked at him. "Please remain lying down for the duration of your transport. Keep your arms and legs inside the gurney at all times. Failure to obey may result in accidental injury."

62 sighed as the Machine turned back around. "Yeah, yeah. I know. I've done this before."

The Transportation Aide pulled 62 through a side door and onto the railway platform. The area was empty. "Where are we going?"

The blinking lights of the Transportation Aide's responders were visible in a crack along the Machine's neck. "You have been injured. Medical attention is required."

"But aren't there doctors in T.A.S.K.?"

"Yes."

62 looked up over his shoulder at the doors behind him. "Then why can't I just see one of them?"

The Transportation Aide ignored the question. 62 probably wouldn't have heard it anyway as the giant doors on either end of the platform creaked open. The familiar screech of the giant transport unit echoed through the tunnel beyond the door to their right. Suddenly the bright headlamp illuminated the void, and the doors widened, allowing the massive engine to pull slowly through the doorway.

The previous two times 62 had seen the transport unit, it had been attached to enough passenger cars to pull groups of Boys. This time there was only one short car behind the massive engine. A single door opened to the platform and the Transportation Aide pulled 62 through the doorway without another word.

Once inside, 62's gurney was locked into place along the far wall. The car was empty aside from 62 and the Machine that escorted him. Not a single chair graced the interior of the car. The door slid shut as the lights shut off. 62 blinked against the darkness as the car lurched forward. 62 could hear the pistons pump slowly in the dark, their rhythm gaining momentum as it began its trek through the dark tunnels to their destination. Wherever that may be.

CHAPTER 12

As much as 62 enjoyed the rail system, traveling in the dark was disorienting. The steady chugging of the engine and clicking of the steel wheels filled the air. The car bumped and swayed as it moved along. The steady rhythm made 62 sleepy, and it wasn't long before he lost track of which direction he thought the train was moving. Being strapped to the gurney in the dark certainly wasn't helping.

He allowed himself to drift into sleep. His imagination came alive and his mind escaped the confines of the gurney. He willed the lights to illuminate above him and pressed his hand to the wall. The crisp lines of reality shuddered. The railway car became pixelated and fuzzy. 62 pushed against the pixels beneath his palm. Dozens of tiny squares floated away from him into the darkness. A smile spread across his face.

62 cupped his hands around his mouth and

exhaled, blowing a gust of wind that pushed the pixels that confined him away. They shattered into a billion tiny squares and fell to his feet. He waved his hands clockwise, and the air around him shifted. The wind swirled around him in a funnel, pulling bits of railway and track high overhead. The wind intensified with every exhale until the moving air thundered in his ears and whipped against his skin.

He splayed his fingers out flat in front of him, palms up, and pushed the bottom of the funnel high into the air. As it moved, the riot of pixels clapped together. Their friction snapped into a blaze of light that shot across the darkness of his dream. 62 made an "o" with his lips and blew. The swirling funnel cloud responded, swishing away from him.

62 realized that the gurney still stood beside him. He leaned against it casually, watching the storm drift. Every so often he'd dream a burst of electricity into existence and watch its sharp fingers illuminate the horizon. The tail of the funnel darted beneath the shock of light, crashing into the ground. Bursts of debris were tossed into the air each time the storm landed. Whole chunks of 62's dream were picked up by the steady cone of wind.

He wished that 71 could be here to see this. They'd once pored over a book together that discussed the theory of air movement. 62 racked his brain, trying to remember what the book had been called. He pressed his hands tightly together, and when he pulled them apart again a small blue book lay between his palms. He turned the book over to read the spine. Introductory Meteorology.

62 flipped through the pages until he found the picture that matched the destructive cone of wind turning

on the horizon. The book called this presentation of air movement a "tornado". 62 got up on the gurney, never taking his eyes off of the pages open before him. He settled in for a quick read, poring over the text. The writer of the book hypothesized that changes in atmospheric pressure could result in a variety of funnel formations. The idea was fascinating and 62 wondered what kind of Man could ever have imagined a time where the air might change.

The pages of the book fluttered beneath his fingertips. He tightened his grip to hold them down, but they flew to life, slapping against one another as if they'd come alive. The book was ripped from his hands as the tornado swept over him and the cover smacked his cheek as it flew up into the air. 62 rolled onto his back and looked up at the storm. Electricity crackled from the head of the funnel, reaching out at him in deadly cords. He tried to lift his hands to push the cyclone away, but his hands would not rise from the straps that now held them to the gurney.

The tiny pixels that the storm carried began to drop from the clouds above the storm. It started as a small tinkle of pieces falling here and there, but they began to drop faster. When they hit the ground, the tiny gray squares bounced along until they found the point where they originated and fixed themselves into place. 62 squirmed on the gurney as they rained down on him, slapping his skin with a thousand sharp points before bouncing away to where they belonged.

The more 62 tried to turn away from the storm, the tighter the straps on the gurney became. The metal frame shuddered beneath him as the wind roared through it and 62 worried that the tornado would carry him away. He forced his eyes open and turned his head toward the edge of the stretcher. He'd lost control of the storm, but if he focused, he hoped he could force the wall beside him to build itself faster. The gurney began to drift, the wheels turning slowly as they rose up off of the floor.

"No!" 62 shouted into the storm. His voice was swallowed by the roar of the wind and the crashing of debris all around him. He forced himself to be calm. Focused on his breathing, counted his breaths until they became long and steady. "You can't take me."

The dream responded. A thousand pixels snapped into place beside him and the gurney shuddered as the mounting brackets on the wall pulled it to them. The storm slowed. It dropped the remaining pixels into place. The funnel dispersed. The whole rail system rebuilt itself in an instant and the force of the world rebuilding itself pushed 62 awake with a start.

62's whole body wrenched against the gurney straps as he tried to leap up from his dream. He panted and shivered, clammy sweat beading on his skin. His eyes darted left and right into the dark until he remembered where he was. The rail car was silent. The Transportation Aide stood dormant, a single red blinking light the only indication that the Machine was still there. It didn't feel like the vehicle was moving. 62's erratic breathing was the only sound, and it echoed in the empty space.

"Hello?" 62 thought he heard the clang of something hitting the rails outside. The vibrating metal calmed so quickly that after a few seconds he decided he must have been mistaken. He looked at the slow blinking light of the Transportation Aide. 62 tried to steady his voice. "I am in need of assistance."

The Transportation Aide did not spring to life. It didn't even turn on. "Aide, I require assistance. Our transport has stopped moving." The only response was the small red light pulsing slowly from the Machine.

62 moved his fingers along the edge of the gurney. He couldn't move much, but he was sure that he'd be able to reach a sensor. They were everywhere. The strap held his wrist tight and he could feel the edge of the thick plastic push into his bones. His fingers were too short and he was too disoriented to find a sensor in the dark.

Something scraped the wall. The squeal of metal on metal rang in 62's ears and this time he knew the sound was real. Something was moving outside. The door shuddered and a blaze of light entered the car through the doorway as it opened. A Machine gripped the heavy metal door. It was about the size of a Man, but it had floodlights mounted to its head. 62 tried to see exactly what kind of Machine it was, but his eyelids forced themselves closed against the pain of the light.

"Please, help me." 62 whimpered. "I am a good Boy. I was injured in T.A.S.K. and I'm being transported to go see a doctor."

The Machine picked something up and put it into the car. Then it pulled itself in. It approached 62 in silence until it gazed down on him from behind the bright lights it carried with it. The heat of the lamps washed over him, drying up the panicked sweat in 62's clothes. His body pressed down into the mattress, nowhere else to go to escape the oppressive intruder.

"I just need a doctor," 62 whispered.

"Well, then, a doctor you shall have." The voice startled 62. It hadn't come from the Machine. A Man appeared at the foot of the bed. He held an arm out toward the Machine and grunted. "Holy dust, you stupid Nurse. Do you think you've got those things bright enough? How about we turn down the lights now that we've found our friend."

The Nurse turned its head, and the floodlights turned with it. 62's vision was overwhelmed with colorful spots when he blinked. Beyond the sparks of color in his eyes, he could just make out the shape of the Man slapping his hands against the Nurse's face.

"I said dim the lights!" The harshness of the light dropped to a gentle glow. "Much better."

62 lay frozen on the gurney. The spots in his sight were fading. The Nurse was emitting some low ambient light and now the Man was digging through a Maintenance bag propped up on the foot of the bed. Shadows masked his face. The Man muttered to himself as he fumbled through his tools, then yelped with glee when he found what he was looking for.

"Are you here to fix the Transportation Aide?" The Nurse with the headlamp produced a tray from its chest and the Man began to line it with tools from the bag. 62 swallowed hard, "Or are you here for me?"

The Man turned toward 62. The light caught the edge of his cheek and illuminated the tip of his nose. The way the light and shadow swirled across his face made the Man's grin look wild. "I'm here for you, of course."

"Please, I have been a good Boy." 62 cried. "Please don't hurt me."

"Oh, 62. It's not going to hurt. At least, not any more than it did before. I mean, there will be a widened potential for error with the system down, but I've fixed these things so many times that I can practically do it with my eyes closed."

62 blinked, forcing the tears out of his eyes so that he could see again. "Like before?"

"Yes." The Man turned back to the Nurse. "Now, you beast. Do you think you could turn yourself into an overhead lamp?"

"Of course, Doctor." The Nurse nodded and reached spindly arms up to the lamps. A whirring sound vibrated in the air. The Machine detached the top of its head and held it up high. With the light source moved, the space around them looked more normal. Shadows were still cast along the edges of the lamp, but the rest of the rail car looked more familiar.

62's eyes went wide. "42, it's you!" A wave of relief washed over him, and he let go of the breath he'd been holding.

42 put his hands on his hips and turned around to look at the Boy. "Well, of course it's me. Who did you think I was?"

"I don't know." 62 grinned. "Some Maintenance Man with a scary Nurse who was going to cut me up, I guess."

"Well, I am going to cut you up." 42 held his thumb and index finger out about an inch apart. "Just a little."

CHAPTER 13

What had once been an empty railway car was now a temporary doctor's office. The Nurse that 42 was working with carried an array of equipment. Once it detached 42's lab gear it looked almost normal. The only thing that looked odd about it was that it still had the top of its head removed. Its arms suspended the Machine's dome from the ceiling to cast light on the room.

62 still lay on the gurney, although the straps were unclasped so he was able to move. He watched Doctor 42 as he rushed around the space and tried to get a grasp on what was happening. "So, where are we?"

42 waved his hand in the air. "We're in the transport tunnels. I'd tell you more, but you have no use for the conspiracy that brought us here. And really, our location doesn't matter. We can't be easily tracked down here. Especially with the power out."

"The electricity stopped?" 62 looked at the Transportation Aide that still sat in the corner. Its red light had stopped blinking. "I didn't know it could do that."

"Well, of course it can. All it takes to stop an electric current is to break its connection. It can happen for any number of reasons. Faulty equipment, the right combination of cut lines. If you sever the system, the electricity has no road to travel."

62 took a deep breath. "But don't we need it to live?"

"Well, yes. The electricity makes all the difference. It's what runs the Machines, the ventilators, the feeding system, the dust-flushing toilets. If the power is out long enough, all the resources will get used up, and we won't be able to survive. Electricity is our life force."

"How long do you think we can live without it?" 62 looked out of the train car into the darkness.

"A handful of cycles at best. Those trapped in their cubes or classrooms would run out of oxygen first. Everyone else would starve."

62's eyes darted back to the doctor. "What's the longest the electricity has been out before?"

42 kept digging through his bag. "Well, that depends on who you ask. The main power plant has, on occasion, been down for dozens of cycles at a time. You'd never know it though, because the back-up plants keep things going." 42 picked up a tiny vial and held it up to the light. "Ah, there you are."

"So why aren't the back-ups working now?"

42 laughed. "Well, it appears that they've been compromised. At least one system has disappeared altogether. There is a rumor going around the labs that the Others took it right out from under Defense's noses."

"The Others?" 62 inched forward on the gurney. The doctor tipped the vial and a tiny chip fell out onto the tray below. 62 recognized it. "Are you replacing my chip again?"

42 nodded. "You're being upgraded. I can't believe I didn't think of this in my earlier research. When I designed the chip you have now, I simply programmed it to output data from another host's prerecorded data set." 42 peered over his tools at the Boy, "You know, from the doctor on Level 2."

62 nodded.

"Well, I'd never even thought about integrating a basic Artificial Intelligence program to filter between live data and programmed expectations." The doctor flailed his hands in the air. "It was so obvious! All I had to do was have it analyze the type of activity you are doing, output your status as normal in real time, and then have the A.I. simply filter the data output for the archives. Whoever is reviewing your data won't know that it's been altered unless they happen to be monitoring you in the moment, and then try look up the same data set at a later time."

"But wouldn't the Head Machine figure that out?" 62 flinched when the doctor picked up his scalpel and waved it in the air excitedly.

"The process is so quick, it won't even register as a blip on the records. The new program replaces your active data so beautifully that there won't be a single trace of the changes." 42 pushed the hair away from the nape of 62's neck and pressed the scalpel against the skin where he knew the old chip lay. "This is going to hurt a bit."

The blade was sharp. Although 62 could feel the cut, the pain didn't register until the scalpel was pulled away. It was hard to resist the urge to flinch. The chip was small, but he could feel it grate against the underside of his skin as it was being removed. The doctor loaded the new chip into a syringe, pressed the needle into 62's neck, and the installation was done. 42 reached his hand back toward the Nurse. "Antiseptic, please."

"Here, Doctor." The Nurse extended its hand and one of its fingers detached. The digit fell into the doctor's outstretched hand.

"Your Nurse keeps falling apart." 62 winced as the pressure on his neck changed with the doctor's movements.

"I've made a few improvements." The doctor held the robotic finger over 62's cut and a drop of wet cream touched his skin. "I've integrated the most important pieces of my lab into the Machine's body. Makes doing house-calls a lot easier than it used to be."

"I thought you weren't supposed to leave your lab?"

The doctor laughed. "I'm not. The only time I can go to my patients is when I'm certain no one knows I'm missing." 42 replaced the Machine's finger. "Nurse, how long until Adaline is back online?"

"Fifty-three minutes, forty-five seconds." The Machine flexed its hand and then began putting 42's tools away.

"Just enough time to get back before life returns to normal. We timed this perfectly. Now, to get you back onto your gurney so that you can go see a doctor for that arm." 42 gestured for 62 to lay down.

"Why can't you just fix it?" 62 looked from the Nurse to the Transportation Aide. "And how is your Nurse helping you if the other Machine's are offline?"

The doctor began the process of strapping 62

down. "Well, I can't fix your arm because I'm not supposed to be here. When you get to where you're going, you've got to arrive in the condition they expect you to be in. And as for this guy," he reached over and tapped the arm of the busy Nurse, "he's been outfitted with a hidden reserve battery. This Nurse can run an extra ten cycles after the last standard Nurse loses power."

"Nine cycles, 23 hours and 58 minutes." The Nurse chirped. "Due to battery degradation."

Doctor 42 beamed, "Of course. I forgot to calculate the battery degradation. How silly of me." He winked at 62 and tightened another strap.

62 watched the doctor and Nurse pack up the last of their tools. He didn't want 42 to leave. "Hey, you said that you can only visit patients when you know it's safe. How did you know the electricity was going to turn off, and where to find me?"

Doctor 42 placed the headlamp back on the Nurse. The shift in the lighting made the peaks of his features glow and the valleys turn dark. His smile became warped in the shadows, like a nightmare creeping out of the darkness. "There's an expression that 71 uses from time to time that goes, 'A little bluebird told me.'"

The Nurse followed Doctor 42 out of the car. The Machine started to pull the door closed, causing beams of light to weave in and out of the rail car. Just before the door sealed shut, the doctor's silhouette turned back. "I hope you heal quickly and rise to the top of your class now that your chip isn't holding you back."

"Hey, wait," 62 tried to catch his friend's attention. The door shut the rest of the way and 62 was engulfed in darkness. He shouted, "What's a bluebird?"

He strained to hear the doctor's answer, but couldn't make out the sound of a reply through the steel walls and heavy door. 62 listened for any indication that his friend was still nearby, but the rogue medical team had already left.

CHAPTER 14

62 fidgeted. Once the power returned, the tram pushed him through the dark to a medical hub. The Transportation Aide moved the gurney along brightly lit hallways and passed information silently to the Nurses that appeared at the end of a long corridor. Every bump, turn and clip of the gurney sent pain bursting through his shoulder. He was glad when the Nurses moved him to an exam room where he knew he wouldn't be jostled.

A hissing sound sprung up around a crease in the wall, which slid open into a wide doorway. A young Man arrived with two Nurses in tow. "Patient appears to have dislocated his left shoulder," one of the Machines chirped.

The Man's long white coat flapped behind him as he threw himself down on a stool. The hover mechanics faltered for a brief moment, dipping down a few inches before it adjusted its calculations to hold his weight.

Without uttering a word he began to unfasten the ties holding 62's injured arm in place.

"That hurts," 62 hissed through clenched teeth.

"It's going to." The doctor's reply was curt and didn't leave much of an invitation for further discussion. The Man pulled the sling off and gestured to one of the Nurses. "Clamp him, please."

The Nurse moved to the other side of the gurney. It placed its hands on his chest and pressed 62 down until he lay flat on his back again. Then it leaned its arms down on his torso until he wasn't sure he'd be able to breathe. "Patient is secure," it announced.

The doctor spun in his chair and waved the second Nurse over. "Repair the dislocation," he commanded. As the Nurse grasped 62's arm, the young doctor turned his back on them and covered his ears.

62 didn't have to wonder why the doctor had his eyes averted and ears covered for very long. The scream that erupted from his throat was long and piercing. The pain that he felt as the Nurses pulled and stretched his arm, and the terrible pop of his shoulder reuniting with its socket was unlike anything he'd ever experienced before. The tendons strained, the muscle throbbed, and then in an instant the procedure was over.

The Man turned back around and touched the offending shoulder. His face hovered over 62, the doctor looking into his eyes for the first time since he'd arrived. "Better, yes?"

Tears splashed against 62's face as he nodded. He wasn't sure if he really did feel better, but he wasn't interested in having the Nurses give his arm another tug. He croaked, "Thank you."

"No need to thank me. The credit goes to the Nurses, as always." The doctor's lab coat slid off of one of his narrow shoulders as he shrugged. The Man slouched back down onto his stool and pushed himself across the room to give the Nurses more room to work. "I'm only here to direct treatment."

The Nurses took turns helping 62 sit upright, resting his affected arm in a new sling. They attached the rigging to a band that wrapped around his chest. "You're the doctor though," 62 said to the Man who now rested casually against a supply cabinet.

"Hardly. Medical Trainee is more like it."

"What does that mean?" One of the Nurses stuck 62's shoulder with a needle. A warm sensation flooded his arm. The pain began to subside.

"I'm practicing to become a doctor." The Man grinned. "You're my first live patient."

62 tried to gauge if the Man was joking. Like most of the Men in Adaline, this one didn't seem to have a knack for humor. "Can I tell you something?"

"Sure." The Man pushed off of the cabinet, gliding across the room on his hover stool.

"Maybe the next time you take care of someone, you could introduce yourself first. Tell them what is wrong and what you're going to do to fix it." 62 took a deep breath when the Nurses returned to their stations at the far corners of the room. Each Nurse docked itself into the wall and went into sleep mode. With their processes silenced, they simply blended in with the rest of the medical equipment.

"Why would I do that?" The Man looked at 62 with irritation.

"It makes people feel better."

The medical student frowned. "But don't you feel better now than when you came in?"

62 wiggled his shoulders a little. Pain throbbed

through him, but it was nothing like what he'd experienced before the dislocation was repaired. "I suppose so, but–"

"Well then I've done my job. Now, keep your arm from moving for the next fourteen cycles. Once the time is up, you can start taking your sling off during training hours. At that point, your Physical Therapy Unit will provide you with approved exercises to help you regain range of motion and muscle tone. In twenty-eight cycles you should be able to stop using the sling completely, although you'll want to keep your injury in mind as you return to full activity." The Man picked up a tablet and wrote notes as he spoke, entering the prescribed instructions into 62's file. Once the tapping ceased, he looked up from the tablet. "Any questions?"

"What's your number?" 62 gave as friendly a smile as he could.

The Man shook his head. "I hardly see the relevance."

"I want to know who you are. That way if I see you again, I'll be able to say hello."

"I doubt we will cross paths again, unless you injure yourself when there isn't medical staff available to repair you. If it matters so much to you though, I'm 574524."

"Nice to meet you, 574524. I'm 1124562."

"Yes, I saw that on your chart." He looked at 62 with suspicion. "Your chart has a lot more notes than the sample charts I've been reading in med training. Do all the Boys have so much medical history?"

62 shrugged. "I don't know. Maybe."

"I think you'd better take better care of yourself, 1124562."

"I'm trying."

CHAPTER 15

When 62 returned to the pod the PTS reminded him that he was unfit to participate in any physical training. Now, 62 stood at the door of his cube and stared through the window at the other Boys as they left. He yearned to go with them and let loose a heavy sigh when the last of his brothers disappeared through the door that led to the arena.

There was nothing to do but rest. 62 lay down in bed, pulled the covers over his head and shut his eyes against the bright light that filtered through the fabric. If he couldn't exercise his body, at least he could exercise his imagination.

The dream came at him fast. There was a rush of wind across his face and when he opened his eyes he was standing atop the rail car. It was speeding down the track at an unbelievable pace. 62 fell flat on his stomach and desperately searched for a handhold as the coach dove into a tunnel. The railway car bucked as it sped through the darkness, shuddering against its predetermined path.

62 forced his eyes open against the wind. He tried to make out the shapes whizzing by, but they were nothing but wavering blurs. The rail car hit a turn in the track, moving too fast and tilting on its wheels. 62 hung in the air for a moment, weightless as the car beneath him pulled away. Then the gravity shifted, the car pulled itself upright, and 62 slammed back down onto the cold steel.

"Stop!" 62 commanded. He pushed his will onto the train and nearly lost his grip when the brakes took hold. All at once the wheels locked. Careening metal slid against the track. The resulting screech rang in 62's ears.

He lay against the cold steel for a moment, catching his breath. As he exhaled, the air in front of him condensed. The metal beneath him felt even colder. Goosebumps prickled along his skin as the temperature dropped. 62 forced himself up off of the roof of the freezing transport unit. He crept carefully, teeth chattering as he peered toward the edge.

62 concentrated. Rung by rung, a thin metal ladder appeared and attached itself to the side of the car. But each time a new rung appeared, the floor below the track dropped another foot. 62 pushed the ladder down to meet the receding floor. The faster the rungs assembled, the more quickly the floor dropped away. Soon he was staring down into a chasm. The steel ladder rungs glinted with the reflection of the overhead lights for a few dozen feet but faded into the darkness of the pit below.

62 took a deep, chattering breath. He swung his legs over the edge of the ladder and began his descent.

As he dropped into the dark, the air became even colder. The cold made it difficult to get a good grip on the ladder. His joints seemed to freeze around the metal rungs and he had to focus hard to flex each finger open and closed. His bare feet were so cold that they burned.

62 looked down, hoping to find the bottom. The darkness of the hole seemed to extend on forever. He considered this for a moment, then pressed his eyes closed. He released his hold on the ladder and pushed away from its safety.

Falling in dreams had been terrifying the first few times he'd done it. Fear was a symptom of being a new dreamer. One who didn't have control of his own imagination. But once 71 taught 62 how to manipulate his body against the rushing air, to glide on the imagined currents and weave through the atmosphere of his mind, the sensation became less frightening. Over the many cycles since 62's first flight, moving through the air had even become enjoyable.

62 flitted through the darkness now. He couldn't see where the wall was, so he stretched his arms and legs out wide. His fingertips didn't touch anything, and his toes only found purchase on the drag of rushing air. He imagined his clothes expanding as they flapped in the air, weaving together to create a web of cloth and string. As threads wove themselves beyond his limbs, the newly-formed pillow of fabric caught the air and held it. Soon 62 was gliding through the air on wings formed from his imagination.

He imagined a place to land. He wanted the area to be flat, soft and well lit. After a moment's concentration such a place appeared in the distance. Light illuminated the landing target from a spotlight hovering in the air. The light faded into the darkness to either side of the new landing pad. Below appeared a pile of giant blankets. 62 shifted his weight against the air and aimed for the soft pile. The stack of blankets grew before 62's eyes, reaching out into the air to meet him.

Despite trying to slow his descent, 62 crashed into the landing pad with great force. He tumbled hard, ripping his thin wings. His limbs caught in the folds and creases of the blankets. When he finally stopped, his whole body was tied in knots. He struggled against the grip of the soft fabric that now enveloped him, but the twisted fibers only gripped his flailing limbs tighter.

"Help!" 62 cried out. His voice was muffled by the cushion of fabric pressed against his face. He refocused, and imagined that he had the loudest voice that ever was. He dreamed that his lungs expanded and became so full of air that his chest puffed out wide when he inhaled. Then he let loose a "Help!" that boomed from his small body. The force of it made the air shiver and the ground below him quake.

"What's the magic word?" A familiar voice whispered.

"Chobham."

62 felt strong fingers grasp his hand. As the fingers touched his skin, the blankets loosened their hold. The hand pulled 62 from his tomb. The light was blinding at first. 62 rubbed his eyes with the heel of his hands. A few long blinks and he was able to focus on the area forming around him.

The blankets turned brown and brittle below his feet. As they degraded, shoots of poa pratensis sprung up from between them. The air lost its filtered metallic tang. 62 breathed deep and his lungs were filled with fresh, clean air. The light above him expanded.

"You've been busy," 71 smiled. The Man let go of 62's hand, only to wrap himself around 62 in a tight embrace.

"I've been stupid." When 62 thought about his dislocated shoulder, it lost the numb mask of his imagination and throbbed with a pain that was incredibly real.

71 smiled. "We often learn our best lessons when we cease being intelligent."

"I prefer to learn my lessons in class." 62 rubbed his shoulder. He imagined the pain fading away. It melted beneath his fingertips and the shoulder became whole and useful again.

"Ah," 71 mused. He began a slow walk through the poa pratensis. "Those are the words of a follower. You, 62, were not programmed to follow."

"I follow you." 62 proved his point by skipping a few steps to catch up with his teacher.

"Hardly." 71's laughter bounced through the dream like a song. "You only pay attention to me long enough to glean whatever lesson you deem to be useful at the time. Then you go off to find some sort of trouble and a new lesson to learn."

62 sighed. "I don't like trouble. I want to be a good Boy."

71 winked. "It doesn't matter if you like trouble or not. It appears that trouble likes you."

62 was reminded of his conversation with the new doctor who set his shoulder back in place. "Do other Boys have medical records?"

"Of course. Everyone has a record. From the time that they are animated, there is a record of their growth." 71 wrapped his arm around 62's shoulders and squeezed. "But I doubt that many have the opportunity to visit medical labs later in life, if that is what you are asking about."

"Do you think it will be mad?" 62 looked to his

teacher, worried.

"Will what be mad?"

"The Head Machine. Will it be mad that I had to be seen by a doctor again?" 62 thought briefly about his first visit to the doctor. He shuddered and pushed the recollection away before the terrifying memory materialized in his dream.

"Oh, yes. Of course all those in power will be disappointed. Adaline has invested a great deal in you." 71 stopped and turned to face the Boy. "Adaline invests a great deal into all of us. It takes a tremendous amount of effort to create us. To feed and care for us."

Anxiety gripped 62's voice as he spoke. "How many times do you think I can go to the doctor before the Head Machine decides I'm not worth it?"

"I don't know." 71 answered. "Let's do our best to not find that out."

62 nodded. The two brothers walked for a while in silence. 62 thought about how anxious he'd been when the PTS discovered the fake readings that his chip was producing. He'd been surprised when Trainer helped to send him to a medical center outside of the training facility. Then, he'd been so scared that someone was going to hurt him when 42 appeared in the tunnels to upgrade him. 62 stopped walking.

"What's a bluebird?"

A breath caught in 71's chest. "Where did you hear that term?"

"42 said that a little bluebird told him that the power was going out and that I needed his help. I haven't ever seen a Machine called a bluebird. What is it?"

"That blasted Man can't keep anything to himself, can he? He wasn't supposed to involve outsiders in this. Oh well." 71 gave a resigned sigh and closed his eyes. He balled one of his hands into a fist. He reached it out in front of him, then extended his index finger as if he was pointing to something.

62 looked at the point on the horizon where 71 was pointing. He couldn't see anything other than the long blades of poa pratensis bending with the breeze. He'd just turned back to ask his teacher what he was pointing at when a small Machine fluttered out of the air and landed on 71's extended finger. 71 opened his eyes and smiled at the thing. He whistled a quick tune. The Machine puffed its chest, then returned the song in a series of chirps and whistles.

62 had never seen anything like it before. It had long, slender panels that wove together to form its exterior. The panels weren't hard or rigid though. Instead, they flexed and danced with the movement of their host. The little thing looked so warm and soft that 62 had to fight an inexplicable urge to reach out to touch it. It stood on two spindly legs and had two large black eyes on either side of its small head. Something sharp extended out from between the eyes; it opened and closed when the thing made the whistling sounds. Its head and back were a light blue color, with a large white patch extending from somewhere underneath. The white seemed to turn to rust under the thing's head.

"This little creature is *Sialia Sialis*. Otherwise known as the Eastern Bluebird." 71 brought the hand that the bluebird used as a perch close to his face. "I learned about them long ago. There was a story about a Man who had many troubles in his life. He met a bluebird and it told him how to solve them."

"What's it made of?" 62 peered closer. The bluebird moved in rapid, controlled bursts of movement and seemed to be in motion even while standing still.

"Flesh and blood like you and me." 71 extended his other hand out to the bird, stroking its belly. The creature chirped in response. 71 extended a hidden panel on the thing and spread it out toward 62. "These are called feathers. They cover the entire body, and when the bird extends its wings, they allow it enough lift to fly."

"I can fly." 62 noted as he reached out to touch the offered feathers.

"The bird is an ingenious design. You and I can fly in our dreams because we can control what happens within our own imagination. But in reality, our bodies are heavy and cumbersome. If you tried to jump off of a desk and fly when you are awake, you would fall to the ground. But a bluebird has no imagination. The way its body is designed, if it existed, in theory it would still be able to fly."

"What would be the point of that?" The bird's body was warm against 62's fingers. It pressed into him as he caressed it, seeming to enjoy the attention.

"That is one of the great mysteries of my imagination." 71 answered. "Perhaps there is no point, other than to make me tell foolish stories."

62 smiled up at his teacher. "They might be foolish, but at least they're fun."

CHAPTER 16

When 62 opened his eyes, he was greeted by the PTS unit standing over him. The Machine's face glowed with flashes of yellow and green. The illumination of the glazed features sent a chill down 62's spine. He inched away from it until his back pressed against the wall beside his bed.

The PTS dimmed and a face projected onto the smooth head. "Hello. It's good to see you."

"What are you doing?" 62 tried to shake the uneasy feeling creeping through his bones. He rubbed his bad arm and the tendons pulsed painfully. The attention of the PTS made goosebumps on his arm that stood so high that he could feel them through the bandages.

"I ran a series of diagnostic tests. A requirement for any Boy who has left training for repair. All functions appear normal. A surprising result."

"You were expecting to find a problem?" 62's voice shook when he asked the question.

"Prior to your accident I perceived a potential abnormality. An irregularity in your data chip." The PTS unit's face went blank. It was as if the Machine was pausing to choose its words and didn't want to give its thoughts away by showing an expression. "It appears that when you took your fall, the delay in your reporting software was corrected."

"Who knew that dislocating a shoulder could be so helpful." 62 shot a sarcastic smile at the PTS.

"Indeed. It appears the gremlins have been knocked right out of you." The PTS nodded.

62 got up from his bed and it disappeared into the wall. "What's a gremlin?"

The PTS displayed a smile and made a tittering noise that sounded almost like a giggle. "Gremlins are a fictitious race. A myth. Programmers use the term for unexplained anomalies in software applications. The phrase spawns from the frustration that they experience trying to locate minute problems in complex programming. It is as if these beings, gremlins, are inside of the Machine overwriting code."

"Do you know a lot about programming?"

"I am a Machine." The PTS turned away from the Boy and stared out of the open doorway with what could almost be interpreted as resignation. "Programming is all I have."

"Are these gremlin things common?" 62's fingers unconsciously rubbed the fresh scar on his neck. When he realized what he was doing, he pretended to stretch the muscles stiffening in his back instead.

The PTS's face dropped. A flash of red sparked across its face so quickly that 62 almost missed it. Its eyes settled into bright orange rings. "No. The anomaly is not common. Those who complain about it are usually incompetent."

62 felt his pulse race and told himself to remain calm. It was a losing battle as his memory replayed his encounter with 42 on the tram. He wondered if 42 had made a mistake with the programming of his chip. If he had, 62 wasn't sure that he'd be able to save either his friend or himself from the Machines.

The PTS's holographic mouth turned back up into a smile and its eyes flitted green. "It appears that either your fall or the recent power failure caused your data to reset. All clear now. Perhaps the chip needed a reboot."

62 shrugged and let loose the breath that he didn't realize he'd been holding. "I don't know about programming, but it sounds like it's a good thing those gremlins corrected themselves. One way or another."

"Don't sell yourself short." The PTS took a step back to give 62 room to remove the tunic that the medical group had dressed him in. When the Boy gave up trying to get the clothes past the attached sling binding his arm, the Machine gently assisted in undoing the straps. "You tested quite high in the aptitudes required for programming. It is likely that were you placed in a programming function, you would do quite well. But then, you tested well in every subject. That's a rarity in your kind."

62's face was so close to the Machine that his breath fogged the glossy skin that encased the hologram. If 62 were this close to another human the moment would be almost intimate. 62 became aware of the cold fingers helping to pull the fresh shirt across his skin. The grip of slender metal hands smoothing the fabric draped over his back made him feel utterly alone.

"My kind?" 62 backed away from the PTS and adjusted the sleeve under his newly strapped arm. The Machine had dressed him perfectly. The adjustments that 62 made to the fabric didn't improve anything aside from making him feel less helpless. "There, that's better."

"I'm sorry," the PTS tilted his head. "By 'your kind' I simply meant animated Boys. They are statistically proficient in a small range of tasks. But your C.A.T. results were impressive across all possible cognitive tasks. The adaptability of your mind is a rarity."

62's skin prickled on the back of his neck. He already felt like he stood out from his brothers in so many ways. But hearing a Machine comment about the scarcity of Boys like him sounded almost like a threat. "Are you suggesting that I'm an anomaly? I'm as good a Boy as any of them."

The PTS raised its arms and waved the palms of its hands in practiced surrender. "Oh, no. Please do not misunderstand. It is a wonderful thing to care for a Boy with such an even aptitude. I imagine the Head Machine has great plans for you."

"The Head Machine? What do you think it will do with someone like me?"

The PTS's eyes flickered orange, then settled back to green. "The Head Machine will ensure that you serve Adaline in the greatest capacity. You will do great things for us, Boy 1124562."

The Machine placed a reassuring hand on 62's good shoulder. The friendly gesture bore a weight greater than the Boy had ever felt before.

CHAPTER 17

By 62's second cycle of mandated rest, he was so bored that he couldn't stay still. He pressed his face longingly against the glass of the closed door and watched his brothers prepare for training. They pulled on their slim-fitting training gear while 62 remained in his tunic; warm, comfortable and cradling the arm that was strapped to his body.

When the last Boy left the pod, 62 kicked the door in frustration. The door rattled on its track and before 62 could get the clamoring metal to quiet, the PTS unit peered in the window.

"Boy 1124562, are you all right?" The Machine's voice was quiet behind the glass.

62 made a show of bending over to rub his foot. "Yes. Just slipped."

The Machine nodded, then opened the door. 62 fidgeted as the PTS leaned over to scan his foot. "There is a slight inflammation under the skin, but I estimate you will be repaired to satisfactory levels in less than ten minutes." The PTS pushed a smile onto its face.

"Thanks for looking at it." 62's bed was locked into place in anticipation of a full cycle of rest. He hobbled over and slumped down on it. "I'll count down the minutes until it heals."

"Do you require any assistance?" The PTS was all programming and wires, but it sounded anxious to help. 62 wondered if Machines ever got bored.

"I don't need anything." 62 rolled over to face his mechanical babysitter. "But I've got to get out of this cube. Is there anything that I can help you with?"

The PTS's face went blurry. It seemed like the programming couldn't settle on a suitable expression and the Machine stumbled in artificial surprise. "You want to help me?"

"Sure. What do you do while you wait for us to come back from training?"

The PTS frowned. "I review medical, performance, and growth data."

62 rolled his shoulder, wriggling a knot of pain free. "That doesn't sound very exciting."

The Machine shook its head. "No. It takes approximately 27.4 seconds to review and catalog the data."

62 cocked his head. "Well I doubt I can help you with that. Seems like I'd only slow you down. What else do you do?"

The tubes in the PTS's shoulders hissed as he shrugged them. "I wait."

"What do you do while you wait?"

The Machine's confused face blurred again. "There is nothing to do but wait."

"That sounds awfully boring."

"I have never had reason to consider the excitement level of my time. I suppose it is boring." The Machine mimicked 62's fidgeting.

62 thought for a moment, then eyed the Machine with curiosity. "PTS, do you think I could take a walk?"

The Machine hummed while it searched its programming for the rules concerning child transit. "A Boy is not allowed to travel through the Training and Skills Kinesiology center without the supervision of a Transportation Aide."

"But if I had an Aide I could walk around a while?" 62 rubbed his chin. "That wouldn't be too bad."

The Machine shook its head. "I am sorry, but a Transportation Aide is not currently assigned to this pod."

"Have you already completed your file review for this cycle?"

The PTS nodded.

"Perfect. PTS, you are going to be my Aide." 62 grabbed the Machine's hand and tugged it toward the door.

"I'm afraid that I have not been programmed to assist with transportation, Boy 1124562." The Machine protested but followed the steady tug of 62's hand. In a few quick strides they'd moved from 62's cube to the main door of the pod.

"Don't worry about it. You're just helping me with my physical and mental well-being. That's in your programming, isn't it?"

"I suppose it is." The Machine nodded. "But we can't go far. I must be in my assigned pod when the other Boys return from training."

"We'll be back before training is over," 62 assured

the Machine. He waited for the PTS to push the pod door open. "We'll be able to see them if we walk around the top level of the arena. There's plenty of room to stretch my legs up there. Plus, then I'll know what I'm missing from training so I can make it up later."

The PTS unlatched the door and 62 started to push it open. Just as the PTS was about to follow 62 over the threshold, the Machine's eyes flashed orange and the unit stopped moving. 62 released the door and it dropped back on its hinges, resting against the hesitant Machine's foot. "This appears to be a reasonable request. I must alert the Head Machine of my change in position. Approval must be received before further action is taken." Before 62 could protest, the PTS's features went dark and the unit became nothing more than a lump of metal in the middle of the doorway, too heavy to move with the strength of one arm and good intentions.

62 felt a wave of panic wash over him. With the PTS slowly folding in on itself as its hydraulic hinges released their pressure, he didn't know if he should stay with the Machine or run back to his bed to hide.

"Brilliant." A voice crept through the crack in the opening.

62 looked through the gap. A body pressed against the door. 62 pushed on the handle to open it wider. A Boy with startling blue eyes stood on the other side. The strange Boy slid in through the open door and hovered over the Machine, careful not to touch it.

"I've never seen anyone shut one of these down so easily," the Boy said. "I'm impressed."

"I didn't mean to. I only wanted to take a walk." 62 couldn't tear his eyes away from the other Boy's face. "Your eyes. They're blue."

The Boy took a step back and covered his face

with his hands. "No! Tinkering rust buckets. Tell me it isn't true. Blue eyes?" He raked at his eyes with his fingers and wailed. 62 moved forward to console the Boy but the blue eyed stranger shrugged him off. When he looked up again, he rolled his eyes. "Of course they're blue, stupid. They've always been blue."

"I've never seen anything like it." 62's hand reached up to touch the glassy blue eyes in wonder. The other Boy smacked his hand away.

"There's probably a lot you ain't seen. And me, too, I guess. So, how did you shut this pile of bolts down?"

62 held his bad arm. "I asked it if I could get some exercise. It said it had to check for permission and turned off."

The blue eyed Boy shuffled his feet nervously. "Not a permanent power down. Means it'll be back soon. I've gotta go."

When the Boy pressed his arm against the door to make his escape, 62 grabbed his shirt to stop him. The fabric ripped beneath his fingers when the other Boy tried to pull away. "Wait! Who are you? How do you live with your anomaly?"

"I'm Bird. But my friends call me Blue for some dumb reason." Bird inspected the tear on his sleeve and growled, "Dang! Do you have any idea how hard it is to get one of these things? This is my last good shirt."

"I'm sorry, Bird. Or Blue." 62's eyes went wide. "Are you the bluebird that 42 told me about?"

"I don't sing a lick, but I know a good story or two. Now let go of me before that thing powers back on and we're both caught." Bird tried to free his arm from 62's grasp as he pulled back through the door.

62 wouldn't let go. When Bird pulled hard again,

62 was thrust forward and his foot got caught in a bend in the PTS's leg. 62 lost his grip, hitting the floor as Bird ran down the hallway. The momentum of the impact sent 62 sliding across the smooth surface, not stopping until he hit the wall on the other side of the corridor opposite the door. The impact on his injury sent a shock of pain through the tissue of his shoulder and made his eyes blur with tears. 62 groaned and rolled onto his back to relieve some of the pressure. He blindly massaged the offending shoulder with his good hand, oblivious to the Machine getting up on the other side of the pod door.

The door swung open on its hinges. The PTS came toward 62 with a red glow in its eyes. "Boy 1124562, you have entered a secure area without permission. You are a very bad Boy."

A small door on the Machine's chest slid open and a thick fog began pouring out.

CHAPTER 18

62 forced his eyes open. Head pounding, he tried to make sense of what had happened. He lay in bed with the blanket pulled up to his chin. His whole body ached. He blinked hard, trying to correct the blurry haze in his vision, but when he tried to rub his eyes he found that he couldn't move. Thick straps held him to the mattress beneath the blanket. His struggle against them was brief; when he moved, the edge of the strap cut into his already throbbing shoulder.

"Welcome back." The strong, deep voice came from the foot of the bed. 62 lifted his head as far as he was able, but he could only make out the top of a Man's head over the curve of his feet under the blanket.

"Who are you?"

The Man got up from where he was sitting and moved to the head of the bed where he stood over 62. The light above them cut around his silhouette, casting his face in shadow. Of course, it didn't matter. All of the Men looked the same.

"Who I am is not important." He leaned over 62 with interest. "Feeling well-rested? That fog put you out for quite a while. Either you're sensitive to it, or you made someone important angry and they upped your dose."

"I feel fine." 62 did his best to smile despite the pounding in his head and the ache in his shoulder.

"Good. Then I suppose you won't mind if I ask you some questions." The Man motioned to the hover chair at the foot of the bed and it drifted behind him so that he could sit down again. "What were you doing outside of this cube?"

62 turned his head, trying to get a better look at the Man now that he was sitting down. He looked just like Trainer, although he wore a long grey coat instead of exercise clothes. He sat up straight and held a tablet in one hand, a stylus poised for note-taking in the other. His movements were clipped and precise. Just fluid enough to be human.

"I don't know." 62 hoped his smile was believable. "It was an accident."

"You don't know, or it was an accident? It can't be both. If you don't know what happened, we will have to send you up a few levels to check your short-term memory functions. If it was an accident, well then, I suppose we need to find the source of the problem to prevent you from having another one." The Man scribbled a short note on the tablet and then looked at 62 with anticipation. "So which was it?"

62's breath caught in his chest at the mention of being sent to have his memory checked. It wasn't all that long ago that a doctor had tried to erase his memory up on Level 2. If 71 hadn't saved him at the last second, who knows what would have happened. 62 was in no hurry to relive that experience. "It was an accident. I didn't know the PTS was going to shut down and I tripped. I fell through the door on my arm. It hurt."

The Man nodded. "Is that all?"

62 nodded. "Yes."

The Man looked down at the tablet and wrote in silence for a moment. When he was done, he tapped the tablet screen to turn it off and slid the device and his stylus into an oversized pocket in his coat. When he looked up again, his eyes were dark and his jaw was tense. "Okay. I wrote down your story for the records. You and I can both feel like we did our jobs in filing the report. Now I want you to tell me what really happened."

"What?"

"I know that you didn't just fall through the door. First of all, there was no reason for you to be out of this cube." The Man snorted. "You're injured. You shouldn't be anywhere near the pod exit."

62 looked at the Man long and hard, trying to decide whether or not he could be trusted. "I wanted to go for a walk."

"A walk? To where? You're in a secure training facility. There isn't anywhere to go."

"I wanted to walk around the top of the arena. Move around a little." 62 couldn't help but wiggle his toes beneath the blanket when he thought about moving his feet along the narrow path that encircled the training area. "I've got to keep my strength up if I'm going to go back to training when I'm better."

"Your doctor told you this?" The Man scooted forward until his knees touched the edge of the bed.

"Well," 62 looked up at the ceiling as he recalled

his instructions to rest. "not exactly. But it makes more sense than lying in bed."

"Did the PTS give you this treatment suggestion?"

62 shook his head. "That thing only tells me what the doctor wrote in his chart."

"Then I fail to see how you came to the conclusion that leaving your cube would be beneficial to your health."

A long sigh escaped 62. He rolled his head so that he could look the Man in the eye. "I was bored, okay? There is nothing to do in here. I wanted to get out."

"So you were trying to escape." The Man shook his head and put his hand in the pocket with the tablet. "Escape is not allowed. Not even for smart little Boys like you."

62 instinctively tried to sit up as he defended himself. The Man's stare did as much to hold him down to the mattress as the unmoving straps did. "I wasn't trying to escape. Like I said, I just wanted to walk around the arena. Then I was going to come right back. I promise!"

"Who helped you disable the PTS?" The Man pulled another device out of his pocket. It was much smaller than the tablet. He set it on the edge of the mattress near 62's head.

"What's that?" 62 tried to get a better look, but the thing was too close to his head. All he could see was a small gray box with a halo of red blinking against the edge of the bed.

"It's a microphone. I may need to reference this conversation later, I am sure you understand. Now, tell me again about the Boy who helped you disable the PTS."

"There wasn't anyone else. It was just me." 62 could feel his face grow warm with the lie. He hoped that the Man couldn't tell. "And I didn't disable it. It turned itself off. I just asked it to be my Transportation Aide."

"So you were trying to reprogram it?" The Man's eyes grew wide. "What gave you that idea?"

"That isn't what I said. I wasn't trying to reprogram the PTS. I just wanted to go for a walk and it told me I had to have a Transportation Aide. The wonky Machine shut itself off when I asked it to be my Aide and take me out of the pod."

"And this other Boy; he was helping you with the programming? To what end? Where were you taking the Machine?"

"There wasn't another Boy. All of my brothers were in training. It was me and the PTS. I didn't try to reprogram it. I just asked it a question!" 62 couldn't help but shout at the Man. The stranger in the grey coat was twisting his words. The blinking red light on the recorder made 62 nervous. Who was listening to them? Worse yet, what would they do to him if they thought he was trying to leave?

A heavy silence filled the room. The Man seemed to be trying to compose himself, and 62 was trying to figure out how to get out of the mess he was in. Neither of them were succeeding. Finally, the Man spoke. "We know there was another Boy. We saw him on the cameras in the hallway. Tell me who he is."

62 let his face go taut, not masking his surprise. "You don't know who he is?"

"If you tell me who he is, I may be able to help you. There are careers for Boys who know things. Good careers." The Man leaned forward, smiling. "There is a lot of adventure possible for a Boy like you. A Boy who can get us the information we need."

"I don't know who he is. He wouldn't tell me his number."

"Of course he didn't give you a number." The Man pulled away, leaning back in his chair with a shrug. "Give me his name, then."

"I don't understand. His name? Boys don't have names."

"They aren't supposed to, that's true. But that Boy does. Tell it to me."

62 shook his head. He couldn't give Bird up to this stranger, no matter what kind of help he was offering. "I don't know what you mean. He was just a Boy. He saw I was having trouble with the PTS after it shut down and offered to help. Then he left."

"Liar!" The Man rushed forward so quickly that the hover chair flew backwards. He bent down over the bed in a rage. His fists landed on either side of 62 with a thud, sending the recording device clattering to the floor. 62 flinched when the stranger's face bore down on him, the Man's nose stopping a hair's width from his own. "You filthy dust-sucker," the Man growled. "I don't care a lick about who you are or how important you might be. I only care about what you were doing outside of this pod with that fugitive. Now tell me who he is!"

62 blinked hard. "I don't know. The PTS shut down and a Boy offered to help. I didn't ask him for his number. I fell and that was it."

"Telling the truth is the duty of any good Boy." The Man stared deep into 62's eyes. His breath sent a tickle of air across 62's face. "So tell me the truth. You were trying to escape. That Boy was helping you. Tell me who he is."

62 felt small beneath the pressing stare. Tears

began to well in his eyes and he could feel his lips begin to tremble. "I just fell. It was an accident."

"You might get another chance to tell the truth someday." The Man crouched down to retrieve his still blinking recorder. He turned it off and slipped it into his pocket. "I hope you take it when it comes. Otherwise, there is a place that they send Boys who lie. Boys who are traitors to Adaline. It's a place you don't come back from."

Before 62 could respond, the Man waved his hand and the door slid open. As soon as he exited the room, fog began to filter down from a vent near the ceiling. 62 knew it was useless to fight against the straps and cried.

CHAPTER 19

62 didn't know how long it had been since the last time he was awake. From the urgent pressing of his bladder, it had been quite a while. One of the wide straps that held him down to the bed sat right atop his belly, making him twitch with the effort of keeping himself dry.

"PTS!" 62's voice came out in a dry rasp. He cleared his throat and peeled his tongue from the roof of his mouth before trying to call the Machine again. "PTS, are you out there?"

The door slid open and the Machine entered. "Hello, 1124562. How are you?"

"Hello. I'm a little uncomfortable. Can I go to the bathroom?" 62 wiggled under the straps to try to get away from the pressure, but they seemed to cinch down even tighter.

"I must record verbal confirmation that you are willing to be a good Boy before I can release you." The

PTS opened a door on its arm and removed a microphone like the one the Man had used during 62's interview. "Do you promise to be a responsible and kind Boy? Do you agree to follow the rules and do your best to keep Adaline's best interest in mind at all times?"

The strap across 62's abdomen twisted and pressed farther into his bladder. He nodded with enthusiasm, anxious to get out of bed. The Machine pointed into the microphone and 62 ceased his nodding. "Yes. I swear. I will be the best Boy you've ever seen. Can I please get up now?"

The PTS leaned over 62's bed. It pressed the microphone closer until 62 could feel his breath splashing off of the microphone and back over his skin with each exhale. The Machine's eyes flashed orange. "Do you promise to avoid dangerous activities and follow all instructions given to you by a Man or Machine of authority?"

62 breathed into the recording device. "Yes. I promise."

The Machine nodded stiffly and retracted the microphone. After putting it neatly away, the PTS tapped the edge of the bed. The straps unlatched and it carefully straightened them before they retracted into the frame. The PTS looked down at 62." You may go to the restroom. You have been asleep for nearly an entire cycle."

62 sat up in bed, body sore. He slowly lowered his legs over the side of the mattress and pinched his side when he stood up. He wanted to race to the bathroom but after all the trouble he was in he thought it would be better to take his time. He shuffled his feet carefully as he moved around the Machine toward the door.

"1124562?" The PTS unit's voice sounded small

and scared.

62 turned away from the door to look at the stoic face of the Machine. "Yes?"

The PTS frowned. "Why did you try to escape from me?"

62 shook his head in exasperation. "I wasn't trying to escape. I really wanted to get some exercise. I can't be programmed to do a job like you are. I have to earn my spot here and I don't want to fall behind."

"The evidence proves that you wanted to give me to that strange Boy so he could dismantle me." The Machine's eyes flashed red.

"I didn't know anything about that Boy when I asked you to go for a walk with me. I don't know who he is or how he got into that hallway."

The PTS's eyes faded to orange, then a cautious yellow. "So you will stay?"

62 shrugged. "Of course I will."

"Good." The glowing eyes changed to green. "Then when you are done tending to your biological duties, let's take a look at your shoulder and make sure that these unpleasant events haven't done any extra damage."

"That'll be great. Thanks." 62 exited his cube while dozens of curious eyes peered through windows. 62 gave an uncomfortable grin as he walked through the common area of the pod, waving awkwardly when he reached the bathroom. 62 felt relief when he finally entered a private stall and could close the door on the world.

CHAPTER 20

"Chobham." The passcode echoed in 62's dream from a faraway corner as he slept.

"Come in," he replied. He pivoted his head left and right to try and locate 71's entry point but couldn't see the telltale break in the edge of his consciousness. A long moment passed without a change in the landscape. 62 got up from the patch of poa pratensis that he'd been resting on and shielded his eyes against the bright light hanging in the sky. "71, are you there?"

A warm hand pressed on his shoulder, but when 62 turned to look behind him, no one was there. He could feel the pulse of the phantom hand through his thin tunic, invisible fingers tugging at his narrow shoulder. A laugh came from somewhere nearby, followed by a teasing voice. "Maybe I'm here, maybe I'm not."

"How are you doing that?" 62 placed his hand on

his shoulder. His fingers hovered over the tunic, a pocket of warm air with the density of bones and sagging skin between shoulder and palm. "I can't see you at all."

71's face slowly appeared, floating in the air above him. "A simple trick of the imagination, Brother. Just as you can make anything appear with your mind, so can you make anything disappear from view. Do you want to try?"

62 smiled and nodded. He scrunched his eyes tight and wished himself invisible. When he opened them again he looked down at his body. It still filled the space it had before. "It didn't work."

71's laugh filled the dream. The rest of the Man's body materialized and he folded his arms across his chest, lifting his beard so it wouldn't get caught between his forearms. His eyes twinkled and his smile made his mustache wriggle. "Try this. Cross your arms, bow your head, and look at your feet."

62 nodded and followed 71's instructions. He looked down at his feet as they wriggled against the long green blades. The poa pratensis tickled his toes and he couldn't help but utter a small giggle.

71 stooped low so that 62 could see him without looking up. "Now, stare at your left foot and I want you to imagine that you only have four toes. Pretend for a moment that your big toe doesn't exist. All you see are your four little toes and the ground beneath where your big toe used to be."

62 looked at his foot. He tried to imagine that his big toe was gone, but it refused to disappear. He squinted his eyes and frowned with concentration, but nothing happened. He pressed his mind and his breath caught in his chest. Still, his big toe wiggled on the end of his foot. Frustrated, 62 blew the breath out of his tight chest and

dropped his hands to his sides. "It's not working."

71 patted the Boy on his head. "Just keep trying; you'll get it. What were you doing before I interrupted you?"

62 flopped down on the lush green poa pratensis and eased his body deep into the bending blades. "I was enjoying not being in pain for a little while."

71 eased himself down beside 62. "Is your shoulder still bothering you? It seems like it should be nearly healed by now."

62 gave a grim nod. "Yeah. Getting in trouble with that Bird Boy screwed it up again. I guess I fell on it pretty hard when they gassed me. It dislocated again. A doctor popped it back into its socket, but now it hurts more than ever."

71's eyebrows danced on his forehead. "What Bird Boy?"

62 rolled over onto his side to face 71. He could hardly contain his excitement. "I met a Boy who calls himself Bird. He has eyes that are bright blue. I've never seen anything like it before. I asked him if he was a bluebird like the one you dream about and he told me he doesn't sing."

62 grinned as he recounted his mistake of trying to get the PTS to take him out for a walk, and then meeting Bird in the hall. With arms waving and heart pumping, he didn't notice 71's face fall in worry.

"You shouldn't have done that," 71 uttered at the close of the tale.

62 frowned. "I wanted to get out so I could keep up with the rest of the Boys. I don't want to fall behind."

"I understand that. Here, in your dreams, it's safe for you to come up with those ideas on your own. But in Adaline..." The Man's voice drifted off and he shook his head. His eyes drifted away and he stared at the distant horizon as he formed his next words. "Bird will only bring you more trouble. Stay away from him."

62 inched closer to his teacher. "You know him. Who is he?"

71 closed his eyes against 62's questioning gaze. "He's a desperate child. He has a screw loose and has been lucky enough to not get caught. Otherwise, he's nothing special. You'd do well to forget him."

"But he doesn't have a number. And the walls didn't scan him. That seems pretty special." 62 nodded in agreement with himself.

71's eyes flew open. They burned with fury. "His kind are a blight on Adaline. They are dangerous and put into jeopardy everything that we've worked to preserve. They say that they want to protect those of us who have the spark of creativity, but then they tear down our systems and steal from us. Your little friend is a thief."

The Man's warnings only made 62 more curious. "There are more like him?"

71's lips pursed. A pregnant pause filled the air before the Man nodded. "There are."

62 lay down on his back and stared up at the deep blue ceiling high above him. "I thought you told us in class that thieves were extinct? That the laws of our Community and planned career systems eradicated them."

"I did. It's a part of our mandated curriculum." The Man closed his eyes again and his voice rasped. "It's a lie."

CHAPTER 21

62 watched his brothers run through the open door toward the training arena for what felt like the hundredth time. He rubbed his injured shoulder with his off hand and closed his eyes when the muscles responded with a deep ache. The PTS had noted a reduction in inflammation but said that it would likely be another several cycles before he could be released to training again. The improvement had initially raised 62's spirits, but as the last sound of pounding feet faded into the distance it seemed like his medical restriction would never end.

As he had every morning since his renewed injury, 62 began to pace his cube. He felt like if he were let loose he could run to the very edge of Adaline. Instead, he was reduced to the steady seven step walk from one end of his cube to the other. It would take nearly a hundred passes before he'd feel a tingle of exertion in his body. He picked up the tempo, pushing himself to complete the task in less time than it had taken the cycle before.

After a while his body began to suck air in more hungrily. His lungs pushed it out in harsh bursts. 62 fought to steady his breath. Though the pulse of his heartbeat against his chest made him feel less useless, he knew that if he exerted himself too much the PTS would come in and try to make him lay down to rest. It was a battle he knew that he'd lose, so he slowed his steps again and waited for the quick thumping of his heart to quiet.

When the drum of rushing blood quieted in his ears, he noticed a tiny scratching noise. 62 stopped mid-stride, trying to figure out where the quiet squeak and whine came from. He cast a glance through the window of his door and didn't see any movement from the PTS. He held his breath and cupped his hand to his ear. The sound stopped. 62 put his hands on his hips. "Weird."

62 started a fresh trip across the cube. He was just about to turn on his heel for the short trek back to the front of the cubicle when he heard the noise again. It squeaked like metal sliding against metal. When he looked up at the vent where the sleep fog blew into his cube he thought he saw a shadow pass over the opening. "What the dust?"

The vent holes were suddenly covered. White fabric pressed against the opening. A muffled grunt came from the other side of the wall, and a loud bang against the grate made 62 jump. When the white fabric disappeared, so did the metal grating that filled the vent. A moment passed, and Bird's face filled the opening. "Hey, there."

62 blinked. He didn't know what to do, so he waved with his good hand. "Hi."

"You got any bots in there?" Bird pressed his eye

and cheek against the opening. His eye rolled quickly through its socket as he peered into each corner of the room.

"Not right now. But I don't know when the PTS will be back." 62 shook his head to knock his stunned thoughts loose. "What are you doing in there?"

Bird laughed. "I took a few lessons recently. Became a Maintenance Man. See?" The Boy pulled his face from the hole and stuck an arm through, proudly waving a screwdriver around in his fist. The arm disappeared and the shadowed face returned. "Had to come down here to help out a couple of friends and figured I'd do you a favor while I was at it."

"A favor?" 62 climbed up on the end of his bed to try to get a better look through the opening.

Bird's face dipped away from the vent again and he pushed a ribbed hose up where 62 could see it. A gaping hole, ragged and uneven, broke the otherwise flawless hose. He pulled the ruined duct back so that he could peer through again. "Now when they try to gas ya, most of that green is going to fall right back here in the maintenance hatch. Just enough will come through that you'll know you're supposed to get in bed and lie there a while. Ain't that neat?"

62 pulled himself back down to the mattress. "This is really bad, Bird. You're messing with the fog system."

Bird's bright smile faded. "I knocked out your night-night gas. Why ain't you happy about that?"

"What am I going to do when someone finds out?" 62 shook his head. "I'm in a lot of trouble as it is. What will they do to me then?"

Bird snorted. "All you numbered kids are the same. Don't know a good thing even if it jumps up and bites ya. Shoot, nobody's gonna notice that anything's wrong with it 'less some tool jockey is back here when the smoke goes off. And then he won't know what's wrong until he wakes up after."

62 wasn't convinced. "Bird, why did you want to do all that, anyway? Aren't you afraid of getting caught?"

"Those bots ain't caught me yet, and I've been comin' down here for a while. Don't think they know how to figure out what I'm up to." The wide smile beamed for a second, then faded back into the darkness again. Bird's eye came back into view and he looked down at 62 thoughtfully. "Didn't I tell you that my friends call me Blue?"

"Yeah."

"Well, I wouldn't go to this kinda trouble for just anybody, you know. That means we're friends."

62 cocked his head. "We're already brothers. What makes being friends worth more trouble?"

Bird's eye rolled sarcastically. "Don't you know nothin'? Friends are better than brothers. Friends are people you choose to trust. You ain't just following orders because some bot tells you to. You see a friend needs help, and you do something about it because you want to."

62 pondered the concept of friendship. Three quick raps sounded somewhere farther up the maintenance shaft. Blue shrugged his shoulders. "Time's up. I gotta go. So are we friends, or what?"

62 nodded. "Yeah, I guess we are."

Bird pulled his face away from the hole and his arm filled the gap again. He shoved his arm through the gap toward 62. His fingers wriggled in the air a moment and his muffled voice called down, "Go on, shake it."

62 stood back up on the mattress and reached out

to shake Blue's hand. "It's good to have a friend, Blue."

When their hands released, the grating went gently back over the opening. The small squeak of metal screws reattaching the ductwork filled the cubicle for a moment and then the air went still again.

CHAPTER 22

The time finally came for the bandages to be removed. 62 asked to walk to the medical center for the final check of his shoulder, but the bots pushed him down onto a gurney for the trip anyway. The procedure only took a few minutes. The doctor's notations on the chart took longer than the exam. Once wheeled back to the pods, 62 leaped from the gurney and rushed over to the PTS.

"The doctor says I can go back to training." He nearly shouted the words, holding back only enough to keep from getting in trouble.

"I have reviewed your records. You may resume physical activity." The PTS flashed a green smile. "Are you happy?"

"Very." 62 raised his arm above his head and waved it in a big circle, rotating his shoulder in its socket. "It feels good to be back in action."

"You'll start with the others during the next cycle. It will be difficult for you to keep up, but I have sent instructions to meter your involvement."

62 shook his head as he walked towards his cube. He stopped in front of the door and looked at the Machine that followed him like a worried Nurse. "I'll try to take it easy, but I'm ready for anything."

"I am sure you are." The PTS's face ebbed from cheerful green to a cautionary yellow. "Before you can begin, there is a Man waiting in the cube for you."

"What Man?" 62 moved to the side of the door and peeked around the edge of the glass window.

"The same one who came to interview you after the incident with your second injury."

The Boy nodded at the Machine. "Thanks for letting me know."

The PTS moved around 62 and opened the door for him. "Please let me know if you require any assistance. Congratulations again on your return to optimal health."

62 entered and stopped just inside the door. The Man reclined in a hover chair, tapping on a tablet while he waited. It was several seconds before he closed the program he was running and turned his attention away from the device.

"Hello, again." The Man got up from the chair and gave a false smile. "Good to see you up and about. This time with proper escorts."

"What do you want?" 62 glanced up at the gas vent at the top of the wall. It looked perfectly normal. No hint that it had been tampered with. He felt his tense shoulders lower just a bit. Hopefully the Man didn't know.

"I heard that you were about to be released back

into training." The Man pulled a small recording device from his pocket. "I wanted to congratulate you on your recovery and see if you had any more information for me."

"Thanks. I don't know what kind of information you want."

"I want to talk to you about the Boy who you were seen with when you tried to escape–"

"When I tried to go for a walk," 62 corrected.

"Yes, well. Whatever you claim to have been doing. That Boy was seen in the area around these pods a few cycles ago, just before a large number of uniforms went missing." The Man paused, waiting for the weight of his implied accusation to sink in. "You wouldn't happen to know anything about that, would you?"

62 glanced back to the gas vent. He realized his mistake and moved his gaze up to the ceiling. "I don't know anything about any uniforms."

"I see," the Man nodded. "And the Boy?"

"Nobody's been in this cube except you, me and the PTS." 62 pointed over his shoulder to the eavesdropping Machine just outside the door.

"You sure about that?"

62 nodded once, silent.

The Man sighed and moved toward the door, pausing to pat 62 on the shoulder as he passed by. "Fine. Make sure it stays that way. It would be a shame for us to lose such a talented Boy due to poorly placed loyalties."

"I'm loyal to Adaline and the Community," 62 parroted the words mindlessly. An automatic response after a lifetime of instruction.

CHAPTER 23

62 panted hard as he lumbered up the steps after his brothers. With the blurred vision of exhaustion, he could hardly make out the bottom of the Boy's feet ahead of him before they disappeared over the top step. He pushed himself up a few more treads, then tripped and landed on his knees. He rolled to his side and lay across the stairs.

"Doing all right?" Trainer appeared upside-down as he leaned over 62's head. He put his hands around the Boy and pulled him upright.

"Yeah." 62 gasped between breaths. "I'll be fine."

Trainer nodded once. "I know you will be. But it'll take more than a couple of cycles for you to catch up. We've been pushing it hard while you were out." The Man's gaze crossed the far end of the arena where the fastest of the Boys had already begun descending the distant staircase. He helped 62 to his feet. "Come on. It's about time for a break."

62 dragged his heels as he followed Trainer back down the stairs. His shoulders slouched more from embarrassment than fatigue. Trainer jogged down to the arena floor quickly, meeting the first Boy in the group of runners. He held his hand up to stop the flow of the group and soon the Man was surrounded by bobbing heads and waving arms as the trainees began a cooldown stretch.

Trainer was halfway through a pep talk by the time 62 made it within earshot.

"... Not one of you stopped to make sure that your brother was all right." Trainer moved his gaze slowly over the flushed cheeks of his subordinates.

One of the Boys smirked at 62. "We're not really supposed to slow down for him are we?"

Trainer extended his arm and waved his hand to beckon 62 forward. He smiled at 62 when he was within arm's reach and placed an arm around his slim shoulders. "This is a tricky lesson to learn. If you were a Machine, then I would say to absolutely keep on going."

With his free hand, Trainer reached forward and pinched the arm of the Boy who'd made the snarky remark. The Boy yelped at the sharp pain. "Since we're not Machines, we have a responsibility to take care of one another. This will be especially important for any of you who move on to Defense and Maintenance. There is an immense amount of time, energy and supplies invested to train and keep us alive. Losing one Man is costly for the whole Community. When you're working, if your brother falls and you fail to pick him up and return him safely home to his pod, you are responsible for his loss."

Trainer's words hung in the air. A cloud of

emotion passed over his face and in a gravelly voice he added, "Believe me, the loss of a brother is not a debt you want to have to repay." The solemn expression only lasted a moment. Trainer soon smiled again. "Now, everyone get hydrated. We're going to take five more minutes to catch our breaths, and then we're heading to the high jump."

The Boys dispersed, each heading to his own pile of towels and hydration packs. 62 wanted to ask Trainer more about what he meant when he talked about owing Adaline for the debt of a fallen brother. But when he turned to ask, Trainer pulled his arm from 62's shoulders and jogged off the field and out of sight.

CHAPTER 24

62 collapsed onto his bed. The last few training sessions had taken every ounce of his energy and he was glad that Trainer had given them the next two cycles off to rest. His tired muscles sank into the soft blankets. He didn't even have the energy to change into a clean tunic before drifting off to sleep.

As soon as the real world faded away, it was replaced by a vision of the arena. 62 stood alone in the vast space. His muscles flexed, ribbons of strength beneath his skin. Without a thought to the pain he'd suffered from when awake, 62 took off running. He leaped over abandoned exercise equipment, bounded up the stairs and was about to sprint across the upper track when he heard hands clapping from the bleachers below. Without fear of losing his balance, 62 skidded to a stop and beamed at 71.

"You are a vision of athletic performance!" 71 shouted across the space. 62 jumped in the air and flew across the arena on an invisible current, landing softly at 71's feet.

"It's a lot easier when you can just imagine that you're the best at everything." 62 sat down in the seat beside 71, his breath calm and steady.

"Of course. If only the rest of Adaline were so simple. Perhaps we wouldn't have so many problems." 71 pondered his own words while 62 pressed his hands together and created a cold hydration pouch out of thin air. "Of course, if everyone could create exactly what they wanted, maybe there would be even more annoyances to deal with."

"If you could have anything that you wanted, what would it be?"

"More time to sleep. The possibilities are endless in here." 71 tapped his temple with his forefinger. "Fewer Machines around telling me what I should pay attention to."

62 nodded. He looked at his former teacher and sputtered, "Well, Blue seems like he doesn't have any Machines telling him what to do."

71 squinted, eyebrows knitting on his forehead. "Oh, his name is Blue now? What do you know of this Blue Boy and his interaction with Machines?"

"Well I think if any of the Transportation Aides could boss him around, they'd keep him out of the supply areas. I don't think they're helping him to steal uniforms."

71 sat up straight and smacked his knee with his hand, causing 62 to jump in surprise. "Blasted bolts! What did I tell you about getting involved with that Boy?"

"It's not like I went looking for him. He just showed up. Afterward, a Man came and asked me about some missing uniforms." 62 couldn't help his mischievous grin. "I don't know what division the Man works for, but Blue sure makes him mad."

"What do you mean, the Boy showed up?" 71 wore a grim expression that made 62 rub the back of his neck nervously.

"I was in my cube. I wasn't doing anything wrong, just resting like I was supposed to. I heard a weird sound and before I knew it the fog vent was loose." 62 looked at 71 with innocent eyes. "I didn't know anything about it. He just did it. We talked a while through the vent and then he left. That's it, honest."

"Did anyone see you together?"

62's hair flopped across his brow when he shook his head. "Everyone else was in training. The PTS wasn't there."

"And the Man? Who is he?" 71 leaned forward so far in his chair that if they weren't both dreaming, he'd probably fall out of it.

62 lifted his shoulders in a shrug. "He wouldn't tell me either of the times he came to talk to me. If he comes back, I'll ask him again."

"He's been to see you twice?"

"Yes. He brings a microphone and records what I say."

71's features went flat, his expression hard to read. He covered his mouth with his hand, gnawing on a finger while he thought. After a moment, he sat back in his chair. "This is bad, Brother. If they think the two of you are in cahoots, this is very bad." 71 turned to face 62. "But how did the Boy find you?"

"Well, my cube isn't that far from the door where he first saw me with the PTS." 62 thought back some more. "And when 42 changed my chip on the Transport, he said a bluebird told him that's where I would be."

71's eyes squinted. "42. You sneaky little..."

71 reached forward and ripped open a seam in the dream. On the other side was a perfect replica of 42's lab, sterile and pristine. 42 puttered away on an experiment in the center of the lab, humming to himself while he worked. 62 always thought it funny that while 71 insisted on creating exotic surroundings, 42 tended to stick with the equipment that he was so intimately familiar with.

42 looked up and smiled. "Hello. I wasn't expecting any visitors. Come in."

"I can't believe you!" 71 barged into the dream, fist pumping in the air. "First, you change the Boy's chip without consulting me, and now I discover you worked with those blasted Others to do it? Do you have any concept of what you've done?"

42's face fell and his hands went up in surrender. "What are you talking about?" 62 followed 71 into the dream. When 42 saw him slip through the opening, his face fell. "Oh, I see. Hello, 62."

71 marched to the nearest desk. He picked up a glass vial filled with purple liquid and hurled it to the ground. The glass shattered into a thousand pieces, liquid shimmering as it spread out across the floor. As soon as the mess settled, the glass reassembled itself, the liquid returned, and the whole vial placed itself back on the desktop. 71 glared at the doctor. "You are so infuriating!"

42 lowered his hands and nodded. "I hear that more and more."

"That Boy has kept in contact with 62. And now Defense thinks that he's helping them steal supplies. How could you tell that criminal where 62 sleeps?"

"I'd hardly call him a criminal." 42 shook his head. "He's looking out for his own best interests, the same as you and me. So what if we help each other out a bit now and then? His talents make a lot of things more convenient."

71 gave a sarcastic nod. "Oh sure, more convenient. Skulking around in dark corners, walking through transport tunnels. You must enjoy pretending you're one of them. You've gone mad, Brother."

62 struggled to keep up with the elder Men's argument. "You think that Man is from Defense?" Both teacher and doctor looked over to 62 with annoyance at the interruption.

"Did he tell you where he was from? Show you any kind of proof of who he was?" 71 spat the words out.

"No." 62 answered in a quiet voice.

"Defense." The Men echoed one another. Each gave a curt nod and crossed their forearms in synchronized annoyance.

"He said there could be a job for a Boy like me." 62 said, eyes growing wide. "A whole career lined out for Boys who could get information."

71 perked up. "He did? You didn't mention that before. Oh, that would be a silver lining. A job in Defense could be a wonderful thing."

42 glowered. "Wonderful for who? The programmers in the Community? The Head Machine and its incessant need for biocide? Sure. Send 62 to work for them. They'll get him all set up with his own private pod and give him permission to murder whoever he sees fit." 42 flapped his hands and raised his voice like a madman. "What a wonderful career for your little prodigy."

"He could help us from within Defense." 71 pointed a long finger at 62 as he glared at his brother. "Bring fairness back to Adaline and end the hunt for anomalies. As he worked his way up the ranks, 62 might be able to make a real difference. Bring things back to the way they were before."

62's eyes bounced from one Man to the other. "What's biocide? What were things like before?" Both Men fell silent. 62 turned his hands up in the air in exasperation. "Well?"

42 was the first to answer. "Biocide is something that we only talk about in the privacy of our minds. It's what we call it when the Machines remove humans from Adaline. When we are destroyed because we're imperfect."

The teacher shook his head. "It's a disgusting term that shouldn't be used at all. Yes, there are flaws in the selection process. But with new leadership in place the selection process could improve. Go back to when the only anomalies that were removed were those visible to the naked eye."

"You think 62 is going to make a dent in the system in our lifetime? You've seen what they do to the Boys in Defense. Those children go into training wide-eyed and full of life. But that's not how they stay. They're brainwashed. Damaged by power without restraint. They'll train our young friend to attack us." 42 shook his head. "And this idea that it's acceptable to destroy the Boys that have something visibly wrong. An anomaly that can be seen isn't any more dangerous than one that is hidden. Those Boys could learn to live among us and serve the Community, no matter how many fingers they have or what color their eyes are."

"The documents from Father clearly state that we are to be identical. Physically indistinguishable in every way. I can't fault the Head Machine for taking its instructions so literally. Who knows what kind of chaos could be wrought with that kind of distraction? Blonde hair, green eyes; it would be our undoing." 71 began to pace, his feet falling heavy on the hard floor.

"They're still human!" 42 boomed. He pounded his desk with his fist, causing the glass vials and steel instruments to chatter across the desktop.

The Men cursed at each other, pointed identical boney fingers at one another and puffed out matching chests. Nothing that either Man said made any sense to 62, and the argument became so heated that he didn't dare enter the discussion again. Although 62 still hadn't learned how to make himself transparent in dreams, the adults before him made him feel invisible.

CHAPTER 25

62 stared at the ceiling between his latticed fingers. He knew that it was late enough that he had to look like he was asleep, but he didn't dare close his eyes for fear that he would be caught in another debate between 71 and 42. There were only a few hours left of the rest cycles that Trainer had prescribed for the trainees, and 62 couldn't wait for them to be over.

His feet itched beneath the sheets, waiting for the opportunity to run full speed across the spongy floor of the arena. His ears ached in the darkness to hear the rush of wind that would come from stampeding down the stairs with the other Boys. The exercise was hard. Excruciatingly painful at times. But the movement provided relief from the thoughts that rattled around his mind when he was alone.

No matter how hard 62 tried to forget about Blue,

something would happen to sling the strange Boy back into his thoughts. 71 warned that he was a dangerous menace. 42 treated him as an accomplice in a secret mission. The intruding Man with all of the questions seemed to think of Blue as a criminal. 62 didn't know which opinion to agree with. To him, Blue seemed like any other Boy. At least, when his eyelids closed over his startling blue eyes.

62 turned his head and strained to hear the PTS moving outside. The quiet whir and hiss of the Machine's mechanics were amplified in the darkness. 62 concentrated on his breathing, making sure that it came out steady and even at a pace consistent with sleep.

A tired yawn fought through 62's practiced breathing and he heard the Machine pause its patrol. The two listened to one another for several minutes before the PTS gave up the silent duel and returned to its work. 62 wondered if the PTS ever wanted to do something more than pace the pod in the quiet rest hours. Could a Machine want things? 42 had somehow corrupted his Nurse enough to have its own opinions. Perhaps the intelligence of a thing could be pushed until it needed more than a task to complete and a place to recharge.

As 62 thought about programming a Machine to have emotions, a tapping noise emerged from behind the wall at the foot of his bed. He unlaced his fingers and moved them from his face to the back of his head, propping himself up to see through the fog vent where a light shimmered and dimmed behind the panel. A tinkering could be heard from somewhere beyond the vent.

"This it?" A Man's voice whispered low. 62 didn't hear a response, but the Man answered anyway. "You sure this kid can be trusted?"

62 eased back onto his pillow. If the voice belonged to the Man from Defense, he didn't want to let on that he was awake. 62 wasn't ready to have another conversation with him or his recorder just yet.

"How'd you pick him out?" The Man's voice faded behind a rustling of fabric. The top of a head shone in the dull light he carried.

"That lab coat upstairs had me track him a while ago." Blue whispered against the vent. 62 could just make his face out as he peered into the room. "They updated his chip. Made him more normal, I guess."

There was a rustling of fabric and another head pushed toward the vent. The light hovering behind the grating painted a pattern of diamonds across 62's ceiling. He couldn't decide which he hoped for more: that Blue and his companion would move along before the PTS came back to check on him again, or that they'd stay so that he could hear more of their conversation.

"Normal." The Man grumbled quietly and turned away. "We've got enough normal around here."

"I saw him turn off a Machine."

The light intensified in the grating and the larger of the two heads pushed its neighbor aside. The Man's curiosity overwhelmed his need to stay hidden. His round eyes bulged through the vent as he looked down at 62. "That kid turned off a bot? Impossible. You know those things ain't got an off switch."

"He did." Blue's voice hissed. "I saw it. He overloaded its program settings and it shut down. Jammed a doorway open. He could'a run away lickity split if he wanted to."

"But he didn't." The Man turned away from the vent again. The light dimmed and turned black as the duct behind the grating was replaced. Footsteps trailed off beyond the wall. The Man's voice came through in a far-off whisper. "Doesn't sound all that smart, if you ask me."

CHAPTER 26

62 wasn't used to hearing someone say he wasn't smart. The words gripped him a little tighter with each breath until his chest hurt and there was a sting of tears behind his eyes. 62 wasn't dumb. The Man that Blue was talking to was just mean. He didn't know that 62 had even scores on all of his aptitude tests, or that he knew how to dream. He might even be offered a career in some kind of secret program. That meant he had to be smart, didn't it?

He rolled over in bed, pulling the covers over his head and shrinking into the dark. The Man thought that he was dumb for not running away when the PTS shut down. That, thought 62, is stupid. The idea of running from the PTS that cared for him was crazy. Who would even think of that?

Then, he remembered. Back when he was in C.A.T. there had been a Boy who ran away. Normally, Boys weren't able to wander anywhere in Adaline without permission. The only time a door unlocked for you was at the exact time you were allowed to go through it. But 1125000 discovered the code to open doors. He'd left his cube in the middle of the night and hadn't been caught by the Nurses until he'd made it outside of the pod. 00 never came back and 62 had always thought he'd been taken away to be punished. But 62 only thought that 00 had been caught by the Nurses because that's what he'd been told. What if 00 had disappeared because he learned to walk between walls like Blue?

62 felt a shiver climb his spine. If a Boy was going to run away, what was there to run away to?

He rolled again, burying his face deeper into the soft threads of his blanket. He slowed his breathing and relaxed his body, starting with his toes. He unwound his muscles one by one until even his nose felt relaxed. A few more measured breaths and he could feel the tingle of sleep enveloping him. Light crept from deep in his mind and a slow falling sensation pulled him into a dream.

He opened his eyes to find himself sitting in a stark, white, empty room.

62 focused on a point in front of him and pushed the air with his hands. A pen entwined itself in the fingers of one hand; a sheet of paper in his other. He wrote himself a quick note. *Where would I run to?* Then he folded the paper in half. He tapped the floor below his feet three times and a small square door opened, revealing a small book. He flipped the book to an empty space in the back and tucked the note inside. When he slammed the book closed, the book, pen and door disappeared with a loud snap.

62 moved to the nearest wall and pressed his ear against it. Not hearing anything, he moved a bit to the left. Then down the wall, over again, and back up until he was standing on his tiptoes. Here he could sense a vibration. There was a faint murmur on the other side and the wall bent slightly when he pressed against it in an effort to hear better.

"Hello? Are you there?" 62 called. He didn't hear a response.

62 closed his eyes and imagined the wall splitting open. The gap was small at first, but soon he could feel air pushing against his face and the murmur grew into the booming voice of 71. He pulled away from the break in the ripped fabric of his dream, slipping his fingers inside and pulling the seams apart until the gap was large enough for him to pass through.

"Can you hear me? I'm looking for Chobham," he shouted. Impatient, he pushed himself through to the other side without waiting for a response.

71 stood on top of a stage. Although he was a small speck on the platform, his voice echoed across every surface. Below the stage sat thousands of Boys. They sat in silence, captivated by 71. 62 started picking his way through the tightly packed crowd. He tripped over someone's foot and only caught himself by grabbing onto the arm of another Boy for balance.

"Excuse me. Sorry about that."

None of the Boys around him broke their gaze from the brightly lit stage. The arm in 62's hand felt cold and it flopped in his grasp like a rubber hose. He pulled himself around to the front of one of the Boys and looked into its perfect glassy eyes.

"Knock knock." 71 boomed.

The mouths of the Boys opened in unison.

"Who's there?"

"Wire." 71 said.

"Wire who?" Thousands of voices returned.

"Wire you asking me? I don't know who it is either."

Laughter ripped through the air. The Boys whooped and hollered, their limbs suddenly able to clench into fists and pound on their knees. Some held their sides, others pointed at the stage and called out for more.

A moment passed and 71 waved his hand over the crowd. The movement caused the group to fall silent and motionless again. He wiped a tear of joy from his eye, and then looked back down at the book in his hand. He read for a moment. Not finding what he was looking for, he began flipping through the pages.

62 pushed forward again. The Boys ahead of him refused to move to the side. Their feet seemed to be planted into the ground. Giving up, he bent his knees and jumped into the air. He sailed over the crowd toward the stage and landed lightly a few feet from 71. It wasn't until the teacher looked up from the book that the crowd noticed him. As the teacher's eyes turned toward 62, thousands of other eyes turned, too.

The attention made 62's stomach flop. He eeped, "Hello. I'm looking for Chobham."

"Hello, there." 71 smiled. "You've found it."

62 was frozen to the stage. He wanted to hide but his arms and legs were locked in place. He'd spent his whole life surrounded by his brothers. But there was something different about being up on the platform in front of them, even if he was pretty sure all of these Boys were fake.

"What are you doing?" 62 finally managed to

push the words through his clenched jaw.

71 giggled and the whole theater laughed with him. He calmed his laughter and waved at the crowd, silencing them again. He gently closed the book he held, a finger trapped in the binding to save his page. He held the thing up so that 62 could see the tattered cover. "I'm joking!"

"You're what?"

"Joking. It is a marvelous mechanism. It's like a short conversation with a bend of humor. The Boys love it."

62 found the strength to turn his head and look over the crowd. The Boys stood as motionless as Machines waiting for a command. Their unblinking eyes stared at 71. "They do?"

"Oh, yes. Well, not these ones so much. They're just here to help me test jokes on for size." 71 opened the book again, bent the corner of the page he was on to save it for later and tucked the book into a fold in his robe. As soon as the book disappeared behind the fabric a quick snapping sound echoed through the space. One by one, the pretend Boys popped out of existence. The sound moved faster and faster through the crowd until it was like grinding gears in an unbalanced Machine. As the last of the Boys vanished, the sound dissolved.

Once the theater was empty, 62 could feel the blood flow back into his limbs. His stomach dropped down from his throat and settled back into his belly, and he was able to bend his arms and wipe the sweat from his palms.

"How do you do that?" 62 gestured out to the empty space. "Talk in front of so many Boys, I mean."

71 tilted his head and smiled. "The same way I do anything. Practice."

62 imagined a chair onto the stage and settled into it. Without the distraction of the crowd his thoughts organized themselves again. "Are you ever good at something right off, without having to practice?"

71 combed his beard with his fingers. "Certainly. I'm pretty good at breathing without having to practice. Although I still find it's a good thing to concentrate on, now and again."

"Not like that. I mean, has there ever been a skill that you've discovered without having to learn it?"

The teacher searched 62 with his eyes, trying to sort out the deeper meaning of the question. "Absolutely. When I was your age, it was discovered that I had a knack for teaching. And so, here I am."

62 slouched in his chair. "Do you remember when 1125000 coded all those doors to open?"

71's face cleared of confusion. He pressed his thin lips together as the memory of the Boy returned. He nodded, silent.

"How could he do that? We hadn't learned much about coding yet. I still don't even know how to open core files up to read unless someone helps me."

71 lifted his shoulders and dropped them down again. "I don't know. He was a brilliant child. The second that basic patterning turned up in his aptitude tests, he understood how it worked. One day he was identifying numeric patterns, and the next he had written an entire set of code that unlocked his tablet." The teacher looked down at the floor and scowled as if discovering a stain on the glossy stage. "I had a copy of everything on his tablet, just like I had yours. I hid the records of his code from the data uploads to the Head Machine to keep him out of trouble. I wanted to see how far he could push the code. What he could do with it."

When 71 looked up again his face was white with worry. "We both know what happened next."

"Where do you think he was going?" 62 thought about Blue, traveling through Adaline using maintenance shafts and empty hallways. He wondered if 00 knew someone like Blue, too.

"I don't know." 71 snorted and rolled his eyes. "Maybe he wanted to explore the parts of Adaline that he wasn't supposed to see until he was grown up. He wrote the code several cycles before his exit. It's entirely possible that he simply wanted to see if his program worked. Or, he may have been brainsick enough to try to get to the outside."

"Outside?"

71 pushed his weight into the floor and the stage erupted into a field of poa pratensis. As the green stalks grew up between their toes, the theater ceiling lightened from gray to white, rising high above them and separating until the white was mere patches in an arc of blue. A breeze pushed warm air around them and 62 could hear running water somewhere beyond the foliage.

"Not many of us can learn to dream," 71 stated. He pulled a fist full of poa pratensis from the ground and shook the soil from its roots. "And most of us can't learn to dream about more than Adaline."

"Like when I started dreaming." 62 remembered, "I only dreamed about the pods and classrooms."

71 nodded. "Some of us have an imagination. 00 certainly had one. The things he could create..." 71's voice trailed off as he stared down at the green blades in his hand. He stroked them with his thumb, lost in an unshared memory. He looked back up at 62. "Sometimes, we forget that our imaginations are make-believe."

"You mean he thought all of this was real?" 62

looked around him. He knew that if he pushed the dream hard enough, he could change the landscape to be whatever he wanted it to be. He could create people, like 71's false crowd, or Machines to do his bidding. Dreams made him feel powerful and gave him control of himself, but at the end of each dream it was clear that none of it was real.

71 sighed and let the green-colored stalks in his hand fade to brown. They became brittle, cracking in his soft grip and dropping in slivers of dust back down to the ground. He held out his empty hand. "I think 00 thought if he opened enough doors, he would find one that opened into a field like this one. There are stories, rumors from troublemakers like your friend Blue, about a place like this that once existed outside of Adaline. Another world. Larger than ours."

62's face twisted in thought. He rubbed his naked toes in the soil and tried to imagine such a thing could exist. He folded his arms into his tunic and rubbed his side. The same side that 71 had tucked his joke book just a little while ago. A spark popped in 62's mind like a new idea being born. He looked up at his teacher. "You've read books about this place. It's how you started to imagine it. Someone showed it to you and you learned it. You didn't make it up."

71 nodded. "Yes, but–"

62 cut the teacher off. "The books had to come from somewhere. Someone knows more about all of this." He waved his hands in the air, gesturing to the scenery around them. "Maybe 00 made it. Maybe he opened enough doors to find the outside."

71 shook his head. His beard wagged and the lush field around them faded. His eyes flashed. "Don't."

"Maybe it isn't natural," 62 thought aloud. "But

we aren't natural either. We're animated by the Machines. Do you think the Machines could animate other things?"

71's hands balled into fists. His voice shook the air as he commanded, "Stop. Stop right this minute. Adaline was created so we could survive. It doesn't create new life, it preserves life. Don't fool yourself into pretending that you can find a way beyond it." 71 shook with frustration. "Do you want to know what's really outside of Adaline?"

62 nodded, his excitement pulsing like static.

"Death. That's all that's out there. The only way to leave Adaline is to die. There's no way to be reborn. We get one life. One chance to become who we are and serve the Community. To leave, to even try to leave, is the end of us." 71 held a sob in his chest. His breath became ragged and his face wrenched in sadness. He took two large strides and wrapped his arms around 62, enveloping him in a protective embrace. "Don't do this. Don't confuse what we are with what we dream to be. I've lost so many Boys to this pretending. I can't lose you."

CHAPTER 27

62 ran the track as ordered. Around and around, one foot in front of the other. Breathing in through his nose and out through his mouth just like he'd been taught. His shins protested with every footfall. A pinch in his side made him lean slightly to the left. Sweat stung his eyes. And yet, he loved to run because he didn't have to think about it. The second that Trainer told them to start running, the footfalls became automatic.

When running was first introduced to 62, he counted his laps. The pain of the run had made him wish he could stop so he counted down laps until there were no more to complete. As the cycles passed, 62 became stronger and better able to settle into stride with the rest of the pack. Now he ran until the PTS at the finish line told him to stop. There was no reason for him to count anymore. 62 knew that if he pushed through the pain, his gait would lengthen and his muscles would stop complaining. He knew that soon he'd feel happy to be running, to feel the wind whisking the sweat off his face. Besides, why bother keeping track of the laps? The Machines were counting them for him anyway.

At times like these, when 62 was able to turn off his racing mind and dissolve into a task, being a Boy seemed so easy. Every minute of the day had an assigned duty. There were no decisions to make. No time spent wondering what would come next. Each cycle had a new list of assignments and as long as 62 and his brothers completed them, everything moved forward smoothly. Of course, 62 couldn't just let life be easy.

As he ran past a wide set of double doors, one reserved for PTS and Transportation Aides, he noticed a bright light shining through the center crack. On the next lap, he couldn't help but focus his eyes on the light. It flickered through the crack at him as he ran by. When he passed again, his feet decided to slow their pace. Since he was going slower anyway, he figured he may as well turn his head a little. He noticed something propping the secure door open, just a few inches. His heart jumped with excitement and pushed him to race around again. The stitch in his side returned just in time for him to slow to a walk, squint at the object holding the door, and see four small fingers wrapped around the edge.

When 62 shuffled by, holding his pained side, a body broke the light shining beyond the crack. A blue eye and a half smile peered out at him. The fingers waved a silent hello, then curled and beckoned him inside. 62 tripped, his left foot wanting to follow while his right foot stuck to its assigned path. He caught his balance just in time, despite thoughts of what might lay beyond the door. He shook his head, trying to separate his desire to explore from 71's warnings that curiosity was dangerous.

Blue took the shaking head to mean that 62 wasn't coming. The Boy shrugged a shoulder and pulled his fingers from the edge of the door. The door drew shut. There was a click of the lock. The other runners whizzed by him with grunts of annoyance. 62 had to force himself to start moving again. To put one foot in front of the other. To breathe in through his nose and out through his mouth like he'd been taught. To will the pain in his side to subside and follow the pack of his brothers as they turned around the gentle curve of the track ahead.

Normally when 62 hit his full stride the pain of his body subsided and his thoughts cleared. But now he had to concentrate on pointing his toes in the right direction with each step. The pain in his side rolled into a gnawing ache to explore. A dangerous curiosity formed as he wondered what lay beyond the crack in the door.

CHAPTER 28

62 squeezed his eyes shut. The light in the common area seeped into his room through the window of his door, distracting him from sleep. It had been a hard day. Trainer had them leaping hurdles placed around the track. 62's body screamed for rest, but the blasted light kept drilling through his eyelids.

He rolled over for the millionth time. The movement yanked at the muscles in his back. His knees shook against the sheets from the effort. He let out a pained sigh when he finally settled back into the mattress. He pulled the sheet up over his head to block the light, but the fabric only rubbed against his nose when he breathed, adding another item to the growing list of things keeping him awake.

As he wondered if he'd ever get to escape into another dream, he heard shuffling coming from somewhere outside his cocoon. A person coughed and the sound echoed in the distance. The fading thrum of sound perked up 62's ears. He didn't bother fighting his curiosity this time. He quickly unwrapped his head from the sheets to take a look.

On the other side of the grate in the wall, a small wavering light filled the darkness. It spilled out of the vent; competing for space in 62's cube, becoming lost in the light tumbling in from the common room. 62 watched the light wiggle around the tight hatch. It grew brighter as its owner settled into a comfortable position in the dark. The dark silhouette of a Boy formed behind the brightness.

"Pssst! You awake?" Blue's voice cut through the silence. The small squeak of screws loosening followed his voice.

"I am. But I'm supposed to be resting." 62 propped himself up on his elbow. He glanced up at the door to the common area. He hadn't heard the PTS go by in a while. It would be coming around again soon. When he turned back to Blue, he hissed, "What do you want?"

Blue pushed the vent cover open a few inches until 62 could see his whole face. The Boy smiled briefly, his raised cheeks trying to mask the sadness in his eyes. "I wanted to talk to you one more time before I leave you alone."

"One last time?" 62's stomach clenched and his heart skipped a beat. He knew he shouldn't want to see this strange, named Boy. He was difficult and dangerous. A friend like Blue would do nothing but get 62 in trouble. A lot of trouble. But he could feel something break deep inside with the thought that their friendship may be over.

"Yeah." The halfhearted smile appeared again. "The doc, 42, told me that you've been talkin' to those goons in Defense. I can't be friends with someone who might tattle."

62 sat up a little more, urged forward in his own defense. "I haven't told them anything, really. A Man came. I didn't know who he was. He knew about you. He said you're bad and asked me to help him find you."

Blue frowned. "And what did you say?"

"How could I tell him anything? I don't know anything about you." 62 shrugged his shoulders.

A nod came back through the grate. "That's how it needs to be."

62 looked around the room, nervous. It didn't matter that 62 was alone in bed, or that Blue was hidden in a hole in the wall. It felt like they were being watched. "So why'd you come back?"

Blue grunted. The sound made it seem that he wasn't sure why he was there either. "Somethin' the doc told me. He said that you'd be on our side if you knew the truth."

The edge of the bed fell away from 62. He hadn't realized that he was leaning forward over the end of the mattress, and when he leaned too far he wasn't ready for gravity's pull. He caught himself just before hitting the floor and scrambled over the loose sheet to regain his balance. His heart pounded against his ribcage once he sat upright again. Both Boys held their breath as they listened for the PTS, or anyone else, to check the cube. They exchanged relieved glances when no one came.

"The truth about what?" 62 finally whispered. His eyes locked onto Blue's, searching for answers to questions he didn't know to ask.

Blue's eyes darted to the door. "The truth about where I live. It's hard for a lot of you Undergrounds to get. Sometimes knowing what's out there makes you crazy." Blue laughed a little too loud and covered his mouth with his hand to muffle the sound. "Look at me. I know the truth and I still come back here anyway, like it's my home."

"You're from here?" 62 pointed over his shoulder to the common area. "From T.A.S.K.?"

"No, dummy. Here, as in Adaline. I ain't lived down here for a long time. Not since the bots first saw my eyes. Long enough to know being trapped down here ain't right. The rest of 'em are smart enough to stay put. But not me." Blue pushed his fingers through his hair. The short strands stood on end, making the Boy look suddenly, terrifyingly, insane.

62's face scrunched. His brain ached. "You... don't live in Adaline?"

Blue laughed again. "That's the look! Happens every dustin' time."

"There isn't anything except Adaline," 62 stated. He was sure that was the truth. It's what he'd been taught since he could understand words. It's what 71 had reinforced. It's all there was. He was positive. Mostly positive.

Blue leaned forward, his face pushing past the shadows cast by the lines of the vent cover. He looked wicked and wild with bright eyes and gleaming teeth. "That ain't exactly right," he crooned. "There's a whole other place. Outside this one."

62 felt the world split. A thin crack formed between what he knew was true and what might not be. Adaline was all there was. But then, he thought back to his time in the classroom. 71 had shown them a picture of the world. Of Adaline. It was square and boxy, sitting alone in the photo. There hadn't been anything else. But wait – there had been something. Poa pratensis had been

in the picture, too. Growing in tufts around Adaline's base. There was a sign posted outside. Outside. The sign was in front of Adaline's boundaries. The sign's feet were planted in the leafy stalks. 62's breath quickened. His pulse rang in his ears. He looked at the wild-eyed Boy leaning through the vent in his wall with new eyes.

"71 says there's no way to live outside Adaline. That everything outside is dead," 62 whispered.

Blue held up a finger. "The doc said to bring this to you. Said you'd know what it was. I ain't met a Boy down here who'd know it, though. It won't grow down here under the lights. You gotta be out in the open where it can see the sky. Then the darn stuff is everywhere."

Blue's voice continued on, but he ducked back into the vent and his words became fast and garbled. 62 couldn't wait to see. He scrambled to his feet, standing on the edge of his bed. It was against the rules, and the PTS was due any minute. But it didn't matter. He had to know.

Blue returned to the opening. He held something in his fist, but it was hard to see it in the dark shadows of the space beyond the vent. 62 reached out for whatever was peeking out from between his fingers. Blue dropped it and 62 watched it fall slowly through the air into his open palm. It was lighter than he thought it would be, weighing less than a cable of the same size would. It was soft and flat when 62 squeezed his own hand around it.

Blue watched in silence as 62 brought his hand near his face, opening his fist to look inside. 62's eyes grew wide. He closed his grip again and jumped off the bed. He rushed to the side of the room where the light shone brightest and held his palm flat again. He brushed his palm with the fingers of his other hand and realized that it was actually three thin pieces stacked together.

The green was brighter than 62 had ever

imagined. The edges of the perfectly straight stalks grew blurry as tears collected in his eyes. He pressed his nose to his palm. The poa pratensis smelled so different from the sterile sameness of steel and plastic of the world he knew. It wiggled in his hand as he trembled; from excitement or fear, he couldn't tell. 62 closed his eyes, held his breath, and pinched the soft flesh of his inner thigh to wake up from the dream.

He opened his eyes. Looked down at his still-open palm. The three green blades were still there.

CHAPTER 29

The door hissed as it slid on its tracks. The PTS stood in the gaping doorway, light spilling around it and making its sharp edges glow. A light in its eyes blinked yellow as it scanned the pod. 62 watched it from under a slit left open between his sheet and the mattress. He was sure that the Machine couldn't see the plant leaves. They were folded in his shirt. The shirt was tucked into his pants. The bundle was hidden under his belly and pressed against the bed. The sheet covered all of him. It couldn't know what he'd hidden. And yet...

The PTS approached him. Its recently oiled joints barely made a sound as it moved through the room. 62's breath threatened to catch in his chest but he knew that the Machine would check his vitals. A held breath would indicate distress. He forced an exhale, even and steady.

The PTS's hands reached out over the bed. They hovered above him. He reminded himself to inhale. He felt the air move through his nose and past his lips. His tongue relaxed more than he intended, vibrating until a snort sounded in the air. He managed not to jump at the sound erupting from his own throat. He evened his breath again. Exhaled. Even and steady.

The PTS froze. It listened for a moment and then must have decided that he was asleep. Its hands retracted. Its shadow faded and the door slid closed once more.

"That was close." Blue's voice sounded far away. He'd seen the movement outside just in time to pull the vent shut, douse the light and duck into the darkness beyond. 62 had been lying on the bed and tugged the sheet over him seconds before the Machine entered. Although getting caught by the PTS would be terrifying, the threat of discovery was also exciting.

62 rolled onto his back and pulled the sheet down just far enough that he could see Blue's face peek out through the grate. "I think you'd better put the screws back. What if that thing had fallen out of place? We'd both be in big trouble."

"You have no idea." Blue shook his head. He produced the screws and slowly turned them back into the back of the vent cover. The slight screech of the metal was like a song of victory being played.

"Why did you bring me the poa pratensis?" 62 fished the plant leaves out of their hiding place. One of the blades had bent when he hid them and he wondered if it could be fixed.

"Well I was hoping it might change your mind about me. And the doc, he was hoping so, too. Well, we want you to be on our side. We've got people to take care of out there. Sure, we can get by on our own. Been doing it since I was taken outside. But it's a whole lot easier to take care of everybody when we've got help from Adaline." Blue's eyes danced behind the slats of the vent in irritation. "And please, stop calling it poa pratensis. For dust's sake, this ain't some stupid class where you have to be proper all the time."

"What do you call it?" 62 tried to bend the crooked blade back to its original shape. He pushed the thin fibers the way he would a bent wire. Instead of straightening, the thing tore in two.

"Outside, it's called grass. And trust me, it's nothing special. It's everywhere. Even where you don't want it to be."

62's eyes went wide. "Why wouldn't you want it everywhere?"

Blue snorted. "There's better stuff than grass out there. Most of the time, the grass just gets in the way of whatever else you want to grow. We try to get rid of it, but it grows right back."

The two Boys sat in silence. One trying to imagine anything more perfect than a field of green grass that reached to the horizon; the other trying to find the words he'd use next. Blue finally found them.

"62, you gotta give those back to me. Push them through the vent and I'll pick 'em up."

"Why?" 62's voice cracked.

Blue shook his head. "If they find you with 'em, they're gonna want to know where you got 'em. They'll be a lot less polite when they talk to you about it, too."

"I can hide it. Besides, if they find it, I'll just say that I don't know where it came from." 62 rubbed the leaves between his fingers. The fibers had little ridges along the leaf. It was like a fingerprint without a finger.

"There ain't any way that somebody is going to

believe you found something like that down here. I'm sorry, 62. I've got to take it back with me." Blue tried to sound tough and protective. "You've seen it, and you know it's real. Now, give it to me. It's for your own good."

62 nodded. He crawled out from under the sheet and stood up at the foot of the bed. One by one, he fed the blades of grass back through the vent. He settled back down on the mattress, folding his legs beneath him. Blue shuffled around on the other side of the wall and 62 imagined him hiding the grass in a pocket, tucked away with a stash of other secrets.

"So, why do you come down here from the outside?" 62 looked at the wall of his cube and tried to imagine anything other than Adaline beyond it.

"To get supplies, mostly." Blue sighed. "It's a lot of work to keep everyone going out there. Getting clothes and meal tablets down here makes it easier. Other than that, it still feels like home. Especially when I find Boys like you."

"What do you mean, like me?" 62 rubbed his sweaty palms against his tunic.

"You know. Kids who don't fit in quite right." Blue shrugged.

"Oh. You mean Boys with anomalies." 62 looked away. "They get rid of us here, if they know. I got taken away once. Almost didn't make it back."

Blue was quiet when he answered. "I know. 42 told me about you seeing a doc and almost getting your brain scrambled. It's part of why he told me to meet you in the first place."

62 raised his eyes back to Blue's. "Why would 42 want you to meet me?"

"He told me you're the only Boy he's ever seen

come back from the brain lab. And you're the youngest Boy to figure out how to give commands to the Machines. He wanted me to meet you so that I could tell you something."

"What?"

Blue's eyes were rimmed with glassy tears. But through the shimmering pools shown a determination that 62 had only ever seen in 71's eyes before.

"He wants you to know that if they ever come for you again, we'll be there."

62 nodded his appreciation, even if he didn't understand. The rest of Blue's words washed over him in a blur until the Boy in the vent said goodbye and disappeared into the darkness behind the wall. 62 straightened the sheet around him on the bed, pulling it over his head where he sat until he was completely covered. Despite his earlier irritation, now he was glad for the light that continued to pour in through the window. Blue was gone, Adaline slept, and 62 lifted his folded leg from the mattress.

He fished the tiny ripped blade of grass from where his knee had been. He held it on the tip of his finger. Even now, in the dim light under the sheet, the green seemed to glow against his pale skin.

CHAPTER 30

    62 closed his eyes tight. It was another several hours before it would be time to get up for training, and there wasn't any better way to pass the time than by entering his dreams. Sleep didn't come easy, though. Every few minutes, 62 dug his fingers under the blanket to check the grass and feel the small fibers. The fear of losing his new treasure, the excitement of having it and the awe that such a thing could really exist kept his eyes fluttering open for another look.

    In time, sleep did come. As soon as 62 felt his head sink into the pillow for the last time, he pushed forward into his mind until he landed in the open space of a dream. He pressed his hand against the floor and grass sprang up in uneven spikes all around him. The grass was less perfect than the way he'd dreamed it before. A new smell wafted through the air, wet and fresh. The texture tickled his feet differently than it had before. Instead of being soft and silky, now individual stiff fibers pressed against his skin. He picked a piece of grass from the ground, relishing the quiet snap of the leafy veins as they broke away from the plant.

Blue told him that he had to keep the grass a secret, but 62 had someone who needed to see it as badly as he had. He pressed his hand into the air, creating a slight opening in the dream. He pressed his face into the opening and looked for 71. It took a moment, but soon he saw the Man sitting in a classroom surrounded by empty chairs. 62 didn't wait for an invitation. He pressed himself into the gap of his dream until it spread wide enough for him to pass through to the elder's dream.

71 looked up from his desk with a smile. "Hello, there. Sleeping well?"

"Not really." 62 jumped into the room. He glanced around quickly. "Is it safe?"

The Man tilted his head and furrowed his brow. "You know, secret passwords only work if you remember to use them. Is something on your mind?"

62 nodded. "Blue told me that he wasn't going to come see me anymore. But then we talked and I think we're still going to be friends."

71's smile faded and the creases around his eyes deepened. "He isn't a good friend to have. I told you, he's a thief and a liar."

"I don't think he's a liar." 62 sat down at a desk in the front row. He closed his eyes and the chair transformed into a giant pillow. He pushed the fluff around until he was comfortable and then settled into the soft cloth.

"Whatever truth he might tell you is simply for his own gains." 71 pressed his hands together, resting his elbows on the desk. He gazed at 62 over interlocked fingers. "He uses information to get what he wants. If he's making you promises, it won't be long before he starts asking for favors, if he hasn't already."

"He hasn't asked me for anything, really. He wanted to know about the Man you and 42 think is from Defense. But other than that—"

"What did you tell him?" 71 boomed. He seemed surprised by the volume of his own voice and cleared his throat. "I mean, it's important that you not share Adaline's secrets with criminals like Blue."

62 was uncomfortable, and he didn't think making the pillow fluffier would help. His skin shivered and his stomach clenched. "He isn't a criminal. He's..." 62 shook his head. "Well, I don't know what he is. Different, I guess."

"He's the wrong kind of different," 71 snorted. "He's the kind of different that gets taken away by Machines."

"I guess." 62 shrugged. "He said he was taken away, but likes coming back. He knows how."

71's eyes narrowed. "What do you mean?"

62 grinned. Finally, he could share his secret with 71. "He knows how to get out of Adaline. He says he does it all the time. And after he's out, he comes back in. Mainly to get supplies, but sometimes just to visit."

"This story of an outside again. Lies. The Boy has a talent for avoiding the Machines, sure. But he's not going anywhere special. Sleeping in vents and maintenance hatches is more like it."

"It isn't a lie. He proved it." 62 held out his hand. Across his palm lay an imagined copy of the three blades of grass that Blue showed him hours before. "He brought me these."

71's beard drooped as he frowned. "Poa pratensis? A figment of our collective imaginations. It's nothing we haven't dreamed a thousand times before."

"He didn't show it to me in a dream. I was awake."

The two friends stared at one another and a heaviness filled the air as the words sank in. 62's smile faded as 71's frown intensified. After several minutes, 71 broke the silence with an agitated sigh.

"A trick. Poa pratensis may have existed once. But its destruction was complete long before either of us were animated."

62 nodded, hoping his enthusiasm would win the teacher over. "It does exist. He brought me three blades of grass." 71 cringed at the plant's common name. 62 ignored the Man's wince and continued. "They were real. I could smell them. I could feel them. They aren't just a dream. They grow somewhere. Some place outside of Adaline."

"There isn't life outside of Adaline." 71 insisted. "If those things are real, they were manufactured in a lab the same as you and me. This story of an 'outside' is just that. A story. A make-believe fantasy that rebellious Men perpetuate to lure Boys away from their innate goodness."

62 slouched low, feeling defeated. He was sure that Blue was telling the truth about the outside. Perhaps it wasn't a wide and wonderful place. But Blue didn't live in the system like everyone else, and he had to be from somewhere. He mumbled, "It's real. No matter what you say, I believe in something outside of Adaline."

71 stood up from his desk. He leaned forward, his usually friendly stance turning hard and menacing. "Don't ever let another person hear you say that. It's against the order of things. A message of crazed anarchy."

Shrinking into the pillow 62 muttered, "I'm not

crazy."

"I know you don't think so. But you're brainsick if you believe in that fairytale." 71 softened, realizing that he'd frightened the Boy. "It's a fantastic thing to want to believe. But there is no proof that life is possible beyond Adaline's bounds. There may have been something there once. There are books that support that theory. But any life outside of Adaline was snuffed out generations ago. Talk of life existing beyond Adaline doesn't help us. It distracts us from the Community, from our brothers and our duty to protect one another. We can't afford to go searching for a world that doesn't exist when there's so much important work to do in the one that does."

62 looked at the grass that still lay in his palm. He let the blades fade into oblivion, erasing them from the dream. It wasn't that he was going to give up believing – there was no way he could do that. But letting the grass disappear was a way to end the conversation. 71 wouldn't believe in exploring beyond these walls. That much was clear.

71 relaxed as the grass disappeared. He eased into his chair and leaned back gently. He squinted curiously at the Boy. "Now that we've gotten that over with, has that Man come back to talk to you again? Getting in touch with Defense would be a great way to clear up this whole Blue story."

"No." 62's mouth tightened. He tried to mask his frustration as he said, "I haven't talked to him. That Man isn't my friend."

CHAPTER 31

Blue's warning about going crazy was well worth remembering. Now that he was curious about where the grass had come from, it was harder to be normal than 62 thought it would be. Difficult to not stare at every closed door and wonder what might lie on the other side. Impossible to keep his thoughts on Trainer's instructions when there was a shred of grass hidden in his cube.

The grass changed as cycles passed, which made it all the more interesting. It lost its glossy sheen, becoming brittle and frayed in the groove of track along the inside of his bed where it was hidden. Tiny flakes fell from it as the color morphed from green to brown. A brown unlike any other 62 had seen. He'd stopped fishing it out of the groove; afraid that if he held it again it might break into a hundred pieces. It seemed so alive when Blue had first shown it to him. But not anymore. The change was slow. Almost invisible. But as the cycles passed, it happened.

"Are you coming?" Trainer's voice broke through his thoughts. 62's vision snapped back into focus. The arena became sharp and clear again. His brothers lined up in rows, sorting themselves by number and stretching their limbs as they prepared for the next exercise. There was a gap in the line where he should be.

"Sorry," 62 mumbled as he stumbled into place. He barely had time to even up with the Boys on either side of him before they were all on the ground. 62 faltered, getting into push-up position half a second too late. It took him until the fifth push to get in rhythm with the others. Then his body took over. Up. Down. Up. Down. Even breaths. 62 closed his eyes, something that none of the other Boys did. His mind wandered. Up. Down. How tall did grass get? Breathe in. Out. Did it bend as it grew? Up. Down. Or did it tear to pieces whenever it was touched, the way the small blade had?

The group rolled to their backs and 62's body followed. He didn't need to tell it to. It knew what to do on its own. His hands cupped the back of his head and his stomach clenched. Up until his nose touched his bent knees. Down to the floor again. Was there wind outside, the way there was in his dreams? Did they have fans outside to circulate the dry air like in here?

62's attention didn't come back into focus until his foot snagged the top of the first hurdle. He didn't remember getting up off the floor or starting his run around the track, but here he was. Flailing his arms as he fell through the air. The floor met his face with hot friction. The gritty rubber grabbed onto his cheek and burned his skin as he skidded forward. A sharp pain stabbed his ankle and he grabbed the injury with his hands.

Trainer loomed above him. "You alright?"

62 rolled to his side. He rubbed his ankle. It throbbed beneath the skin. "I'm fine."

Trainer helped him to his feet. "You've got to keep your head in the game."

62 looked up, worried that Trainer knew what he was thinking. The Man had helped him before, but that didn't mean he wouldn't turn 62 in if he broke the rules now. He looked at the hurdle toppled over on the ground behind him. The brush of his foot against the rail had been just enough to make it lie down. It looked like it was resting while all the other hurdles stood up, doing their job.

"Do you need me to get that looked at?" Trainer kneeled beside him and took the ankle in his hands. His fingers squeezed, looking for an injury. 62 pulled his leg back.

"No, thanks." 62's voice was sharp. He could feel the twist inside the ankle and rubbed it with his own hands.

Trainer stood up. His fingers moved to rest on his hips. "Well then, get up and walk it off. Do a lap at standard marching pace, then two at a jog. When you're done, get back here and finish these hurdles."

A few cycles ago, 62 would have followed Trainer's command immediately. He would have limped his way around the track on a sore ankle until the sharpness of his fall wore into a dull ache that could be ignored as he bounded over hurdles. That's what the Machines of Adaline created him for. To follow directions.

62's hands stopped trying to rub the soreness out of his ankle. His eyes shifted away from Trainer's impatient gaze to the double doors shut tight behind him. The same doors where not long ago, Blue had been.

Where light had shone down an unexplored hallway.

"I don't want to."

The words came out on their own. Trainer looked as startled at the admission as 62 felt in voicing it. The other Boys made it around the track again, the pack leaders bounding over the hurdles. They each took awkward steps around the hurdle that still lay face-down on the track, casting sideways glances as they trotted past Trainer and 62 on their way to the next jump.

Trainer's face squished. His head turned sharply from left to right and a grunt escaped as he processed what 62 said. "What does want have to do with anything? You'll complete today's tasks."

"No." 62 rolled his weight onto his hip and got his good foot under him. He stood and straightened his clothes. He tested the twisted ankle. The pain was sharp. "If I walk on it, it'll hurt. It's not bad enough for medical, but it will be if I keep running. I'm going to sit for a while."

The strained look on Trainer's face faded. It was replaced by frustration. His arm shot out, fingers clasped around 62's elbow. "You will get back on that track and do as I've said."

A quick tug and 62's elbow slipped through the Man's grasp. "Why?"

Trainer's eyes went wide. "Because I told you to."

62 turned to watch 1124621, one of the slower Boys jog past. Slower? He was running twenty seconds behind the leader, and that made him inferior. His form was perfect in almost every way as he detoured around 62. But because his left foot had a slight drag along the pavement at the start of each step, he'd never make it to the front of the pack. It was a slight variation on a perfect step. The drag created by thousands of steps made each

day added up to him never being able to make it to the lead. An anomaly so slight, it was debilitating.

62 understood Trainer's increasingly rigid stance. The Man was trying to be perfect. To be seen as valuable, he needed to have perfect trainees. They all needed to meet the mark because some other Man or Machine said so. Trainer didn't have a choice. He had to make 62 run because it's what he was made to do. But that wasn't 62's fault. It was Adaline's fault. It was the gears that weren't supposed to stop grinding; systems designed not to fail. If 62 didn't get back in line, Trainer would have to answer for the error.

But 62 didn't have control over that. Trouble was going to come down on them both because he'd fallen in the first place. Trainer would have to explain the delay that had already happened. Justify the imperfection of a distracted Boy failing to clear a hurdle.

62 shook his head. "Sorry. I'm not running any more today."

Trainer's hands balled into fists. His mouth gaped open and closed as 62 began to walk away. He pushed out gravelly words once he tempered his anger enough to speak. "If you walk away from this track, I won't help you when they come asking about you. I don't care what the others say. You aren't special. You're just another anomaly."

62 shrugged. "I understand. You can't do anything else. But I can." He turned away with a proud smirk and a sore ankle.

CHAPTER 32

The exhilaration of walking out of the arena was quickly replaced by panic. 62 wasn't sure what he'd expected to happen, but it wasn't this. The hallway was empty when he passed through the exit. No Transportation Aide waited to escort him back to the pods, and when he neared his cube the PTS was nowhere to be found. The common area was flooded with a quiet like he'd never heard before. No whirring fans in the overhead vents. No clicking of Machines passing through on their errands.

When he reached his pod, both the doors to it and his cube were open. The automatic door had slid shut behind him when he'd left for training earlier that cycle, he was sure of it. He crept toward the cube's open maw and stopped short when he saw feet resting lazily on the floor. The attached legs crossed somewhere around the corner, just out of sight. They were Man-sized and had an air of patient waiting even as they unfolded and recrossed into a more comfortable position. 62 held his breath and tried to decide whether to enter, or run.

"There's no point in loitering." A calm voice called. "You may as well come in, I know you're there."

62's feet moved before he was ready. He passed the threshold and found the Man from Defense leaning back in a chair, studying his hands. The Man didn't look up when 62 entered. Despite the tight quarters, he didn't bother to tuck his legs under the hover chair. 62 stepped cautiously over them as he made his way toward the bed.

"What's going on?" 62 asked after settling onto the mattress. He looked for the Man's recording device but didn't see it anywhere in the room. That didn't mean it wasn't there.

"It's my understanding that you've finally made a decision." The Man's voice was cool and even in a way that made 62 shudder.

"A decision about what?"

The Man's eyes wandered up from his cupped hands. "A decision about where you're going next."

62's spoke slowly, carefully choosing his words. "I guess I did. I hit a hurdle in training and twisted my ankle bad." He straightened his leg out in front of him as if the Man would be able to see the pain that throbbed under the skin. "I told Trainer I needed to sit for a while. I'll try again tomorrow."

"That's not exactly how things work." The Man's gaze drifted back down to his folded fingers. "We aren't designed to self-diagnose. If you don't have a note from medical on file, then technically you're fit to jump a thousand hurdles. As far as your trainer is concerned, you're engaging in some extreme laziness."

"I've been hurt before. I know what I'm supposed

to do to take care of myself." 62 tried to sound confident. The throbbing of his ankle evaporated as a wave of anxious adrenaline pumped through his veins.

"You're right. About being hurt before; not about having the power to dictate your own treatment." The Man leaned forward in his chair and raised an eyebrow. "If I understand your file correctly, you've been to Medical a few times, haven't you?"

The question sounded more like an accusation than an inquiry of concern. 62's tongue went dry and his mind went blank. He nodded in silence. His hands moved down to his ankle and he massaged it absently. The pain of the twist returned with new force. It was as if his leg was getting ready to leap off the bed, and his ankle was trying to communicate what a bad idea that would be.

"In fact, you've been to see the doctors with more frequency than any other Boy in your animation group."

62's tongue worked itself loose and his voice croaked. "I have?"

The Man nodded, mimicking 62's wide-eyed nod a moment before. "Do you know why I think that is?"

"No."

"I think someone's coaching you. Causing you to have accidents so that you can move around Adaline with more freedom than you're allowed. I think you've been helping them. They're just using you of course; but I think they've tricked you into feeling like they're helping you, too."

For the first time during their conversation the Man's fingers flexed. His palms flattened and he held one out so that 62 could see what he'd been protecting. Lying scattered across the mature, pale skin were the brittle, brown pieces of 62's grass. "1124562, I think you've been a very bad Boy."

CHAPTER 33

"I can help you." Although the words spoken were quiet, they sucked the air out of the cube. They echoed in 62's mind long after they were spoken. The Man continued to speak but his voice was drowned out by a rush of suffocating panic.

The Man turned his mouth into a smile. His cheeks plumped and lips curved in a way that would seem reassuring if it wasn't for the sharpness of his eyes. The false kindness was an expression of power that drained 62's courage until a shiver ran down his spine and goosebumps speckled his arms. 62 watched, unblinking, as the Man pulled a small bag from a pocket. He unfolded the bag one-handed, careful not to drop the shreds of grass folded in his palm. 62 focused enough to read the word EVIDENCE as it fluttered on the front of the waving bag. The Man tipped the hand holding the grass into the bag and flicked the tiny fibers in. The bag made a sharp sound when the Man removed a long strip of protective plastic from the lip of it. He folded the top over to seal it, and then held the bag up to inspect the grass again through the two layers of sealed translucent plastic.

62 blinked back tears. "How?"

"How what?" The Man raised an eyebrow as if he'd already forgotten everything he'd just said.

"How can you help me?"

"It's not just about me helping you. We can help each other." The Man leaned forward and put a heavy hand on 62's arm. His hand was warm in a way that wasn't comfortable. The heat built until it burned. "We both need answers and we can work together to find them. You help me to find the dust loving idiot who brought this filth into Adaline, and I can protect you."

62 pulled his arm away from the Man's grasp. He edged backward along the mattress until he rested against the cold wall. He imagined that he could feel the sensors scanning his skin through his clothes and shuddered. "Protect me from who?"

As if on cue, a Transportation Aide appeared in the still open doorway. It stood large in the opening, eyes flashing orange. "We are ready to move subject 1124562," a mechanical voice ebbed from an unseen speaker.

The Man shook his head and raised a halting hand. "Not yet. I'm not done. Wait outside." The Man waited for the Machine to turn away and nodded in its direction. "I can protect you from them."

62's eyes drifted from the unnumbered Man to the Machine that waited just beyond the door frame. "Where are they taking me?"

"They want to take you to the other side of Adaline. It's not very pleasant there. Lots of Machines who try to get inside your head." The Man pointed a finger to his temple and turned it in a small circle as if his hand was a drill probing for data. A dark and knowing look passed over the Man's face. "Oh, that's right. Your file says you've gone up the chute to the labs before. Although this time you won't be sent to the idealists on Level 2 that think they can reprogram erroneous little Boys. There's no coming back from where they're sending you."

62's eyes bulged. He remembered vividly being in the small room. The straps that held him down to the table pulled at his arms and legs. The memory seemed so real that he could feel them digging into his skin. His breath became short and clipped. Nurses gazed over him while they explained to an evil doctor that the side effects of a reprogramming procedure would likely kill him. 71 had saved him then and found a way to bring 62 back to class with a new chip and a stronghold over his own thoughts. That all seemed so far away from where he sat now. 71 told him to help the Man who tucked the bag of evidence into the folds of his clothes.

"What do I have to do?" 62 didn't bother to whisper. If the Man hadn't recorded their conversation, the Machine outside surely had.

"Instead of going up the elevator with them, you can come down to Defense with me. It's safe there. Comfortable, even." The Man leaned back in his chair, arms crossed as he looked around the cube. "Better than this place, anyway. I have authorization to push you straight into our advanced recruits team. After a trial period, you could be working with Men a generation ahead of you."

"Working on what?" 62 leaned forward. The thought of a comfortable cube was much more enticing than another trip to the lab.

"Our focus is to find the criminals who steal from our people and corrupt their loyalty with rumors that there is an outside. They're like a virus. They spread fear and uncertainty to Boys and Men alike, weakening their logic enough to believe such a ludicrous fantasy."

"I don't understand. You think the outside is a fantasy?" 62's eyes searched the Man's hands. "But what about the grass?"

The Man shrugged. His eyebrows scrunched and he raised empty hands in the air. "What grass?"

"The grass that..." 62 pointed at the Man's side pocket.

"If you agree to come with me," the Man cut in, "then nobody will know that you had anything to do with grass. I have the authority to wipe your file. You come with me, and I can write a report that you found the illegal substance and reported it like a good Boy. I can say that you found it stuck in a vent. You help me find the outlaw that brought the contaminant into Adaline, and together we can create a future that is long and productive. But if you don't come with me right now," he pointed out into the common area where a second transport unit now waited beside the first, "I'll let them bury you under every scrap of data in your file until there isn't a Man or Machine that can save you."

"I don't know." 62's eyes flicked from the Man to the bots beyond the door. He trembled, unsure what the right answer was. He knew that 71 would encourage him to work with Defense. But Blue was his friend, too. 62 trembled, mind racing.

"I think I know someone who can help you decide." The Man stood up and moved toward the door. There was a murmur of voices in the common area and then the Man walked through the open threshold and disappeared.

A Boy 62's age entered the cube. His movements were smooth and controlled in a way that made 62 feel self-conscious of his own gangly arms and wobbling legs. The other Boy's hair was cropped short. His expression was dark. He sat down in the hover chair across from 62's bed and stared at him.

"Do you know who I am?" The new Boy asked. His words were smooth and deliberate.

62 shook his head, his own mop of hair brushing across his forehead. The similarity between each of his brothers made all of them seem familiar and this Boy was no different. He had the same deep eyes and pale skin as the others. But the way this Boy carried himself was altogether different.

"I'm called Boy 1124999."

CHAPTER 34

62 leaped off of the bed. His arms wrapped around 99's neck and his head rested on his brother's shoulder. Tears of joy spread across his cheeks. "You're here. Alive. I never thought I'd see you again."

99's arms remained folded in his lap. His shoulders went rigid, a startled grunt the only response to 62's emotions. When he did move, 99 shifted backwards and loosened 62's grip. "Yes, I'm here. When Major asked me to assist in recruiting you, he didn't tell me I should expect such an extraordinary welcome."

"Major?" 62's head turned and he gazed on the now closed door. "That's his title? He never told me who he was." 62 took a step back from 99. His hand still rested on his brother's shoulders as he appraised him at arm's length. His voice dropped to a whisper. "You came to recruit me. You work for Defense?"

99 gave a nod. "I had an anomaly when I was younger. Some referred to it as a gift. But it made me feel

different. It made me disobedient and wild. I was on a path that would have ruined my life. Much like the path you're on now."

62 pulled his hand back. He sat down on the edge of the bed. He looked with sorrowful eyes at the emotionless face of the Boy who had once been his closest companion. "We were friends, but you didn't tell me about the dreams. I didn't find out until after they took you. I wish I'd known."

99 raised a hand in the air and shook his head. "I only told one person. I only told him enough to get approval for cognitive repair. It's been said that he encouraged me to explore the anomaly, but I don't remember the particulars. Sometimes I wish I'd learned more about my curse. Maybe the Man who encouraged me would have had some answers. I can't remember him now." 99 rubbed an invisible pain on his temple. "The doctors did their best to fix me. They were successful in clearing my memory, but the dreams remain. The Major saw my file before I was removed from C.A.T. and found a way for me to use my dreams to serve a greater purpose. A way to use my curse to help the Community."

99 rose from the chair, standing at his full height. His square shoulders and jutting chin made him look older than 62, even though the Boys were the same age. 99 cast an emotionless glance down at 62 as he shrunk into his bed. "I was given a second chance, then. Now I've come to pass that chance on to you. Boy 1124562, if we were truly friends, come with me. Help me to set Adaline right. Together, we can make this world better for our brothers. And ourselves."

In the first motion of friendship that 99 had made, he extended his right hand down toward 62. His fingers hovered in the air, waiting for 62 to make the next move. The two Boys looked into each other's eyes for a long while.

    Blue was a good friend and would be hurt if 62 abandoned him. But 99 was more than that. Even if 99 didn't remember, 62 did. They were closer than friends. 99 was his brother, and he loved him above all else. 62 reached his hand up to meet 99's. Their palms met and fingers grasped in a firm handshake. While their skin melded in the warm clasp of agreement, 99's eyes brightened. For an instant, he looked like the same brother that had worried over 62 in the passageways of C.A.T.

CHAPTER 35

The railway platform felt crowded despite there being only one Man and two Boys queued for the next transport. Transportation Aides stood in tight formation around them, forming metal walls that 62 was too short to see past. The Machines' lights flashed yellow and green, processing data even though there was no movement on the platform aside from the inhale and exhale of their human companions.

"Where are we going?" 62's voice came too loud in the tight group.

Major looked away, gazing over a Transportation Aide. His eyes searched the empty tunnel to his left. 99 smiled slightly. "Home."

The three didn't exchange any more words. The air filled with the screeching sounds of wheels on rails. Metal clanged and the engine hissed as their transportation unit fought its way to a stop. The passengers boarded, the doors clamped shut, and the engine surged forward again.

62 lost his bearings as soon as they pulled away from the platform. He could feel the seat beneath him surge to the left. Moments later he braced himself as the vehicle stopped at another, much smaller, platform. The doors opened and 62 fell into line behind 99 as the group exited. This platform would have felt small had he been standing on it alone. With everyone else, they had to stand shoulder to shoulder, chest to back, and arm to metal in order to fit without having anyone topple over the edge. The group waited in uncomfortable silence for a long while until 62 heard the familiar sigh of metal doors sliding open somewhere out of view.

"We'll be right behind you. Stay in formation until we arrive." Major's voice was unmistakable. As soon as his command was issued, the Transportation Aides each moved forward on their hydraulic limbs, filling what 62 recognized as an elevator box.

The elevator doors slid shut. A quiet ding marked the elevator's movement, and the Man and two Boys breathed in a sigh of relief.

"It gets a bit crowded, moving prisoners." Major remarked. 99 nodded in response.

62 flushed red. "Is that what I am? A prisoner?"

Major shrugged. "As far as the Community is concerned, yes. You've broken the law by aiding criminals. You've kept contraband in your cubicle and ignored the commands of your trainer. Any one of those things would be a mark against you. But combined, it makes you look like a growing threat."

"What's going to happen to me?" 62 glanced around, nervous. The drop from the edge of the platform was only a few feet, but if he tried to run there'd be nowhere to go. Following the rails would either lead back to T.A.S.K., or get him lost.

99 placed a reassuring hand on his shoulder. "You'll go to trial. But when you tell them that you are going to join Defense, and swear to use your knowledge to help Adaline, they'll allow you to be rehabilitated. The Community needs Boys like us."

"I don't understand."

Major squatted down on one knee, making himself level with his two companions. "There's an old saying. 'It takes a thief to catch a thief.' It means that in order for us to understand our enemy, we need to become our enemy. Right now, the biggest threats to Adaline are Boys and Men who seem normal on the outside, but who have anomalies in the way they think. We need Boys like you, who think differently from the rest of us, to help us to identify those threats."

62 took a step backwards, feeling unsteady under the weight of the camaraderie around him. "And what happens when you find them?"

A small ding sounded and the doors at the mouth of the platform slid open, revealing an empty elevator box. Major stood up and gave a smile that made 62's stomach churn. "We give them the opportunity to rehabilitate, or be removed from Adaline permanently. The same option we've given you."

CHAPTER 36

Defense looked almost the same as the other areas of Adaline. The only difference was, everything was spotless and orderly in a way that made it look like no one worked there at all. This wasn't the case, as evidenced by Men walking with purpose through the open spaces. But it was clean in a way that made 62's skin crawl.

"This way." Major swept an arm toward a set of chrome doors, polished so thoroughly that it looked like the trio would walk into their reflections. The doors slid open when the approaching group was just out of reach and 62 decided that must be how they avoided the smudge of fingerprints. Major led the way into the brightly lit room. Inside the open double doors stood a row of beds. Just beyond, Nurses plugged into charging stations lined a wall. 62 stopped dead in his tracks when he noticed the straps and wires dangling from the edges of the beds.

99 pushed past, giving a rough bump to 62's shoulder as he went by. The Boy and Major walked together toward the far bed. 99 climbed onto the mattress and reached for a cap with a series of connectors that lay on a table beside him. Major pressed buttons on a box nearby and one of the Nurses sprung to life. While 62 remained rooted to his spot just inside the closing doors, the Nurse began attaching cables to 99's cap while he adjusted the strap below his chin.

"What is this place?" 62's voice cracked when he was finally able to push out the words.

The Nurse's eyes blinked yellow as it processed the question while its arms kept moving. It helped Major tie 99 down to the bed after connecting the final cables to the Boy's head. "Hello, Boy 1124562," the Machine chirped merrily. "Welcome to the Dream Ward. My data load states that you will be assisting us today. Please, choose a bed and make yourself comfortable."

62 took a step back toward the now-closed doors. They didn't sense his approach as he moved closer and remained tightly sealed. This side of the door was missing its chrome polish. Instead, 62 reached behind him and touched the smooth, white finish of the right door. If the door had sensors, it wasn't picking up his signature. He lifted his palm, leaving a foggy smear on the otherwise pristine finish. As he stared over his shoulder at the unmoving pair of doors, his hand print shrank. The change was almost imperceptible at first. The fingers began to thin and the edges of the palm print started to fade. A moment later, there was still a small circle where the heel of his hand had rested against the cold surface but the lines that marked his fingers had dissolved to lines no wider than a strand of hair.

"They're self-healing." Major's voice sounded just

behind 62's ear, making him jump. "You can't see them, but there are billions of microscopic Machines cleaning away the smudge. These doors could be shredded into a thousand pieces, and those little bots would simply piece them back together."

62 stared at the newly cleaned door. Although the finish didn't hold the shine of the reflective chrome outside, it was clean enough that he could see the outline of his silhouette in the door's panel. Major put his hand down heavy on 62's shoulder. "The Machines are perfect, you know. Each one knows its place and performs its function without question."

The pressure on his shoulder told 62 that Major wanted him to turn around, but he didn't move. "We do that, too."

"Most of us," Major's fingers tightened on 62's shoulder and he pulled the Boy to face him. "But not all. Pick out a bed. It's time to get started."

62 nodded. He chose the bed next to 99, who already lay down with his eyes closed. A second Nurse approached, wordlessly attaching 62 to a contraption matching the one affixed to 99's head.

"You said this is a dream room?" 62 directed the question at Major, but it was the Nurse who answered.

"Dream Ward."

"What's a dream?" 62 let the question hang in the air. Major looked up from the panel he was studying and raised an eyebrow.

The Nurse's eyes fluttered from green to yellow. 62 thought he saw a spark of red, but the color was gone before he was sure. "A dream is a function of the human brain, wherein thoughts and feelings are cataloged, reviewed and altered creatively."

"It's an anomaly." Major cut off any further reply

the Nurse might have given. "It was a lower brain process used by primitive Man. When it was discovered by the Head Machine, it was removed from our mental synapses."

"You think I have this anomaly?" 62 looked over at 99, who continued to lay unmoving. "Does he still have it?"

Major nodded. "Affirmative on both counts. We've picked up unusual brain activity from you before. The records show that in the past you've had many of the same idle brain patterns that 99 had when he began suffering from the dreams."

62 pushed a bit further, unsure of how much of himself to give away. "But my brain scans now- are they okay? Or is there still something wrong with me?"

Major looked back at the panel and turned a few dials. The cap on 62's head seemed to shrink, sucking itself down over his hair. "Your data has been fairly average, overall."

62's shoulders slumped in relief. The chip that 42 implanted must really be working. "So why bring me here then? If I'm normal?"

Major's eyebrows furrowed. "We've found that once the anomaly is present, even if it's corrected itself somehow, it can be activated again."

"But why would you want to force an anomaly?" 62 lay down on the bed at the Nurse's guidance. "I thought the whole thing about anomalies is that they're bad. Shouldn't you let me stay normal?"

Major stood at the head of the bed and leaned over. His face was upside-down from where 62 lay, his features distorted by the white lights overhead. "I understand if you're nervous. Especially given your past experience up on Level 2." Major's teeth shone bright despite his shadowed face. "Honestly, if you wanted to stay in the general population so badly, you would have learned to behave when you were given the chance."

62 struggled as the Nurse strapped his left foot to the bed. "I want to talk to Trainer. I'm a good Boy. Let me go back."

Major's shadow lifted as he moved away from the bed. When he returned, he held a tablet above 62's head and angled it so that he could see a grainy image of Blue running down a maintenance hall. A string of Men and Machines raced soundlessly after him. Blue rounded a corner at the end of the hall. The pursuing crowd on his heels disappeared in the same direction. "If you were a good Boy, you would have told us about this little dirt muncher the first time he approached you."

"Ready," the Nurse's voice chimed.

Major stood up and tossed the tablet on a nearby table. "Light him up."

CHAPTER 37

"I don't see him." 99's voice crept in from somewhere far away.

"Vitals are normal." A Nurse's voice chirped quietly. "Rapid eye movement has engaged and the brain stem is active."

"Dustbuckets." Major's voice was louder than the others. Something poked at the side of 62's head.

A metallic smell drew nearer, followed by the pulsing sound of hydraulics. "1124562, please confirm if you are awake."

"I – I don't know." 62's voice seemed to be coming from somewhere outside of himself. Beyond the darkness. He tried to open his eyes and look toward the trickle of voices, but no matter how hard he tried, they wouldn't open.

"What was that?" Major sounded frantic. "Nurse, can you confirm a response?"

62 was cold. Much colder than he remembered

being just a moment ago. He tried to move his hand. Pain screamed up his arm, but the fingers wiggled. Looking down, he could almost make out his limb in the dark. He strained against the pain again, and his hand came closer. But it wasn't attached to his body. It just floated in front of him on its own, sending shocks of electricity through him every time it shifted in the air. Hands couldn't just glide out into open space. This wasn't real. He was dreaming.

62's voice trembled. "Where am I?"

"I don't know." 99's quiet response was definitely coming from somewhere outside of the space 62 could see. "I'm on the starting platform, but I can't see you."

62 understood. His teacher taught him to block his dreams from the prying eyes of others and the privacy had become second nature. He pressed his mind forward, concentrating in the direction his brother's voice had come. "Can you keep talking? I might be able to find you if I can hear you."

Major's huff threw 62 off course. "I can't believe they sent another dud. Nurse, begin detachment procedures."

"No!" 99's shout seemed to come from two places at once. "He's in the dream with me. He says he can hear me. Don't unplug him."

"Confirm instruction," the Nurse peeped.

"Maintain dream sequence. Keep platform loaded until 99 confirms contact."

"Can you tell them to shut up?" 62 shouted. He stopped trying to unravel his dream. The outside voices were too distracting.

"62 requests radio silence until he gets his bearings." 99's words entered in stereo once more. One voice coming from somewhere in 62's head, the other coming from the lab beyond the dream. Then 99's voice shifted, becoming singular. "If I stop talking aloud, can you still hear me?"

He nodded before he remembered that 99 couldn't see him. An arc of electricity shot through 62's neck. "I can hear you in the dream. Does it always hurt this bad?"

"Yes." 99's voice was as sad as it was distant. "They're activating our anomaly using a computer interface. The electrodes stimulate our dream processes."

62 pushed forward. The darkness surrounding him swirled to gray. As it lightened, he could just make out the form of a Boy standing alone in the distance. "I think I see you."

The figure shifted. Its head turned. "I see you, too. It looks like you're coming in through a wall. I don't know how we got separated. That's never happened."

"You've done this with someone else?" 62's vision cleared. He stepped through the air until his feet touched the sturdy billet steel platform.

99 nodded, expressionless. "I'm not allowed to go alone."

"Who do you normally dream with?"

"You know those beds in the Dream Ward?" 99 took in a deep breath, letting it out with a whoosh before he spoke again. "They all used to be full."

Major's voice boomed overhead. "99, have you made contact?"

"Yes." Both Boys spoke in unison.

"Good. Let's see what he can do. Nurse, load up the dream sequence." 62 felt a pat on his head, Major's action of approval pushed pins and needles through his skull.

As 62 flinched, 99 shrugged and offered a weak

smile. "You get used to it."

When the shooting pain cleared, so did 62's vision. The landscape had transformed. No longer were the Boys standing on a lone steel plate hung in the air of their consciousness. Now their feet were firmly planted at the platform of a transport unit. The sound of its whistle screamed toward the Boys seconds before the white light of its headlight crept out of the tunnel.

"I've been here before," 62 said. "This is the platform outside of T.A.S.K."

"Are you sure?" 99 mused. "I think you'll find it's a bit different."

The walls fell backward, the ceiling lifted, and beyond the edge of the concrete, grass shot up from the ground. The transport's brakes hissed and squealed as it came barreling out of the mouth of the tunnel to the Boys' left, which now protruded from a mound of dirt instead of a brick and mortar wall. To their right, the tracks rose up in the air. They assembled in the sky, then drifted down to the ground, settling just above the waving grass in the distance. When the screaming of the tram's brakes stopped, the passenger car doors opened.

62 shifted his gaze from left to right, taking in the transformation. They were in a field, so much like the fields of the dreams he shared with 71. It was breathtakingly beautiful; almost beautiful enough to make the shooting pain in his limbs fade.

"Have you ever seen anything like it?" 99's eyebrows arched quizzically.

Deciding that it would be in his best interest to play dumb, 62 shook his head. "What is all this stuff?"

"It's a dream." 99 grinned. He took a few steps forward, entering the waiting rail car. He turned, looking back at the platform where 62 still stood. "You coming?"

CHAPTER 38

The transport unit clattered on tracks strewn through open fields. It slowed as the scenery changed from grassy knolls to industrial steel. A Man sat atop a pile of broken Nurses. A moment later the air turned thick and gray, making it difficult to see a Boy running through a stream of hydraulic fluid that had ruptured from a cracked pump just outside. Down the tracks a bit farther another Boy threw buckets of dust into the air. Coating himself so thick in the gray particles that he looked like he'd been born of cement instead of flesh and bone.

62 took in each scene. He recognized the elated look of freedom on the faces of the figures as they passed by. He'd experienced the same thrill of discovering there were no rules when he first learned to dream. He also understood the limitations of each of the figures as they skittered by the trembling glass. None of them had ever been shown how to imagine beyond the objects right in

front of them.

"How did you learn how to make the start of the dream so different from Adaline?" 62 turned to his brother.

99 shrugged. "Another dreamer showed me the field once. I liked it, so I kept it as a part of my dream. It's a place I can go back to when I enter and exit others' dreams. Helps me to not get lost."

"Another dreamer? Was it one of the ones the beds in the Dream Ward were made for?" 62 frowned. "Where did they all go?"

A sadness drew itself across 99's face. "Yes. It was one of them. Most of them were removed from service. Major says that spending too much time in dreams makes a Man forget what's real and what's not. Something about how pretending gets into our heads and makes us stop following the rules."

62 nodded. He'd had difficulty falling into line himself because of how suffocating it felt to be awake. Looking out the window, he saw a Man in the distance fighting a PTS unit. From the Machine's bent arms and leaking hoses, it appeared the Man was winning. 62 pointed at the incident as it faded into the distance. "Are you imagining all of these things?"

"No. These are the dreams that are happening in Adaline, right now." 99 sat up straight and glanced out the window briefly, then slumped back down in his chair. "We're supposed to monitor and report them."

62 left the window, moving across the car to sit down next to his brother. Slumped as he was, 99 couldn't have seen the group of Boys gathered around a cascading shower of cleaning fluid; splashing in the resulting puddles and spraying one another with smiles on their faces. "Do you report all of them?"

99 shook his head. "The others did. They reported everyone, whether they were dreaming about breaking the rules, or not. Major caught most of the ones that were reported, and their dreams disappeared."

"What happened to them? The ones you worked with before."

"Four of my partners on the Dream Ward found out that the other three had been letting smart Men go. Doctors and programmers, mostly. Men who were using their dreams to create new systems for Adaline. The last time we all dreamed together, there was a fight. They wrecked one another's consciousness. Horrible things said. Worse things done."

Silence crept between the Boys as the rail car clattered on. The transport unit began to slow and the air filled with the hiss and squeal of brakes being applied to metal wheels. The door at the end of the rail car opened with a slight whoosh of escaping air. 62 sat quiet beside 99 until the he rose from his seat. Staring straight ahead, 99 whispered, "There were eight of us then, but only five of us woke up. I was left alone since I was still in training, but the four who survived were removed from service for the attack."

"Where did they go when they were removed from the Dream Ward?"

99 turned his face toward 62. Tears welled in his eyes. "They were sent to the lab to have their anomalies taken apart and studied. If they wouldn't help us in the dreams, then they had to be useful some other way."

62 remembered the threat that Major had issued on his arrival to Defense. He breathed a deep breath, letting it out again slowly. "Well, I guess I'm stuck here with you, aren't I? I was almost someone's experiment once and I sure don't want to do that again."

99 chuckled, his eyes dark. "Doesn't sound fun at all. Let's go."

The Boys stepped through the tram door and into a classroom. This one was larger than the one that 62 had attended in C.A.T. Desks formed a semicircle in long sweeping rows. 62 half expected 71 to be standing at center stage, perfecting one of his new jokes. Instead, a young Boy played with blocks on an instructor's desk in the middle of the room.

"Hello." 99 called into the empty room.

The child's smile beamed. "Want to play?"

99 nodded and began weaving his way past the empty chairs. 62 followed, unsure what such a small Boy was doing imagining himself out of the Nursery.

"What game are you playing?" 99 pushed a chair to the desk and plopped down. He pulled two scattered blocks back into the pile.

"Build and crash." There was a high-pitched squeal. "You brought someone to play with!"

99 nodded. "Yes. This is 62. He's our brother."

"I'm Pi." The child pointed at himself seriously, then squealed and fell into a fit of laughter.

99 rolled his eyes. "He's 3141592. Somebody thought it was a good idea to start teaching him math early and he figured out that if he put a point behind the 3, he could call himself Pi."

"Pi, Pi, my little eye. I like math and I like Pi."

62 couldn't help but laugh. "That's an easy way to remember your number."

Pi's laughter ended and he began stacking the blocks as high as he could reach. When he got to where he needed to step on his tiptoes to keep placing blocks, 99 picked him up and helped him reach a little higher. They were down to the last block and the tower wobbled precariously over them. Pi and 99 strained to place the last piece.

"Let me help." 62 touched the tower, imagining it being firm and steady. The shaking ceased. Then he took the block from Pi and covered it with his other hand. "One, two, three." Opening his hands, he revealed that the single block was now a group of three identical cubes. He tossed the blocks in the air, and guided them atop the tower with his mind. The stand of blocks didn't even shudder as the last pieces were placed.

"How did you do that?" 99 asked. In his distraction he dropped Pi to the floor a little too hard. The smaller child didn't seem to notice.

"That was amazing! Can you show me?" Pi leaped toward 62, clipping the edge of the desk with his shoulder. Both Pi and the tower came crashing down, the Boy squealing with joy as blocks rained down around him.

"Sure, I can show you." 62 grinned. Pi scooped up some blocks and thrust them back onto the table. 62 stared at the remaining blocks on the floor and willed them to rise up, sorting themselves by color in a neat line along the edge of the desk.

"Maybe some other time." 99 placed a tight grasp on 62's forearm. "Pi, I came to see you tonight because I need to know if the bad Boy has come to see you again."

Pi frowned. "But I want to know how to make the blocks pick themselves up."

"Not now." 99 insisted. "I need to know, Pi. Did he come to see you again?"

"Maybe." Pi turned away, ducking behind the desk in a slumping pout.

"Did he bring you anything?"

"No." Pi's voice trembled.

A quiet snapping sound made the two older Boys turn. It was a small and intermittent sound. It took the Boys a minute to search out where it came from. One of the chairs in the far end of the room appeared to be growing. Its color shifted from silver to deep green. Long, leafy tendrils emerged, unrolling themselves along the surface and reaching toward the ceiling in a search for light. The quiet sound intensified as the grass grew thicker. Longer.

Pi gasped, peering over the corner of the desk. "I didn't mean to do that!"

99 nodded. "Thank you, Pi. That's all I needed to know."

CHAPTER 39

62 and 99 sat on the edge of their beds, eyes locked. Both wore a frown of discontent.

"Well?" Major hovered expectantly. "Did you find anything about the thieves?"

"They're recruiting." 99's voice was flat. "They've shown our contact in the Nursery foreign matter."

A heavy sigh escaped Major as he slid his weight down to the edge of one of the beds. He slumped down beside 62. "We were supposed to have stopped it by now. How far do you think they've spread?"

99 broke away from 62's gaze. Sliding his eyes up to Major's face, his mouth danced between a defeated frown and an angry grimace. "I don't know. I'm not sure how they found dreamers that young. We almost didn't find Pi, and you told me where to find him because of his Nanny. Maybe they're accessing the Boys by physically entering the Nursery."

"A Nanny told you about him?" 62's voice

cracked.

Major nodded. "The Machines compile reports around the clock. If there's strange data collected, the units are programmed to alert the system. Works like a charm, unless someone messes with the data stream."

62's replacement chip itched under his skin. He fought to keep his face straight and his hands in his lap. "How do you know if someone's messing things up?"

Major squinted. He wasn't used to anyone asking so many questions. "We just do."

"Well Pi's Nurse is reporting normally," 99 injected, breaking the tension. "Maybe the thieves have a way to read the data logs."

Major waved a hand in the air, dismissing the comment. "Impossible. Adaline's security can't be breached."

"But you said that these bad guys might be in the Nursery. Isn't that a breach?" 62 couldn't help but ask.

"You are not cleared to discuss that." Major turned to 99 with hopeful eyes. "Any new dreamers to report?"

99 shrugged and shook his head. "Pi's the only one we found." Major sighed. "He isn't the ideal subject for 62 to observe. I hope you come across a new anomaly so you can show him what he'll be expected to do."

62 considered all of the dreamers they'd passed in their dream. "99 explained the reporting requirements to me. I think I understand the basics."

Major's eyes squinted again. "You two are dismissed. 99, please have a full report of your progress by the end of the cycle. Make sure you include whether you think 1124562 will be a help or a hurdle to the program."

62 waited for 99 to hop off his bed before he

followed. Major had already started pounding the buttons on the computer before the Boys had left the room. 62 glanced over his shoulder at the Man who cursed under his breath and kicked a Nurse in frustration. The door opened as 99 approached, and 62 had to hurry to catch up before the doors locked him inside the ward again.

"Where to now?" 62 tried to make his voice sound excited and hopeful despite the thick dread filling his stomach. He followed 99 down a hallway, around a corner and into an oversized room where a Man sat behind a large desk.

"I'm going back to my pod to write my report." 99 waved at the Man as they entered. He lifted his chin and spoke over the edge of the desk in a stronger, more certain voice. "Major says he's done with 1124562 for now. His cell assignment should be on file."

The Man nodded and tapped some buttons behind the desk. Before 62 had time to question what was happening, two Machines larger than any he'd seen before came lumbering into the room. They were broad and intimidating. "Correctors, take him to cell seven," the Man instructed. The two correction units nodded in unison, their red eyes passed over 99 and settled on 62.

"We'll let you know when we need you again," 99 called as 62 was taken away. "It takes Major a while to get through paperwork though, so it might be few cycles."

62 let the bulky metallic arms carry him through the room toward a set of heavily reinforced doors. There was no point in struggling. His choices were clear. 62 could either go along with whatever Defense wanted to do with him, or fall to whatever fate the other dreamers had faced. 62 may not know what was in store for him here, but he knew that he wanted to survive.

CHAPTER 40

62 lay on the floor of the stark white cell. The small room wasn't any more uncomfortable than his cube had been when he was back at C.A.T., but it hadn't taken long for him to realize how accustomed he'd become to sleeping on a soft mattress. The lights dimmed, signaling the end of the cycle. 62 rolled on his side, pulled his blanket over his head and closed his eyes.

He rubbed at his neck. His fingers passed over the spot where his chip had been removed and replaced. Not once, but twice, 42 had cut him open and given him the gift of normalcy. He wondered how long it would take for Major to suspect that his readouts weren't correct. He already knew that someone was tampering with the system. It felt like only a matter of time until they found out he was an imposter. An anomaly within an anomaly.

Forcing himself to breathe deeply, 62

concentrated on the darkness of sleep. He could feel his limbs loosen; feel the sensation of falling down through the floor and into nothing. The beeps and shuffle of the correction bots faded away until 62 felt free and alone in the darkness. This void was soothing and vast, so unlike the black oppression of the mechanically forced sleep back in the Dream Ward. He tightened his already closed eyes and focused on Pi. It hadn't been that long since they'd left him playing with blocks. Maybe he'd still be there.

The familiar tear in the edge of his consciousness separated. He pressed his face against it, looking first with his eyes at the white light beyond and then pressing his ear to the gap and listening for Pi's voice.

"One, two, three." A small voice creaked from some distant place. An exasperated gasp. "I want the blocks to fly. Why isn't it working?"

62 pressed his fingers into the gap and pulled the edges of darkness apart. Once the opening was wide enough, he poked his head inside. There, sitting on the ground in an otherwise empty room was Pi. The child held a block in his palm. He closed his fingers around it and covered it with his other hand. "One, two, three!" Opening his hands, the same block rested in his palm, lifeless. Frustrated, he tossed it to the ground and stomped his feet.

"Need some help?" 62 pushed the rest of the way through the gap, folding it closed behind him.

Pi's eyes grew wide. "How'd you do that?"

"It's just a trick of the mind." 62 patted his temple with his forefinger. "A friend showed me how to dream up all kinds of things. Even how to share dreams with people I know."

"But there wasn't a transport." Pi looked left and

right, flummoxed by the solid walls surrounding them. "You can't just pop up. Oh, you must be pretend."

"Do you have pretend people in your dreams very often?"

Pi considered the question, then nodded ever so slightly. "Sometimes."

"Well then, I guess that's what I am. Just pretend." 62 bent over and reached for the block on the floor. Before picking it up, he looked over at Pi. "May I?"

Pi beamed. "Oh, yes! I remember this part. You're going to turn it into three blocks, and then make them fly."

"Maybe." 62 turned the block over in his hand. It doubled in size. Pi's eyes went wide. "I was wondering if you could tell me about the green stuff that grew out of a chair earlier tonight."

Face scrunched, Pi turned his nose up in the air and crossed his arms. "I'm not supposed to talk about it. Even to pretend people like you."

62 nodded. "I was just wondering who gave it to you, that's all." He set the block down on the ground at his feet and pinched the top of the square. Its corners rounded. He pulled and pinched, stretched and pushed the block until it was a blob nearly his own height. Then he inhaled and blew his breath over the pale surface. It melded into the shape of a Boy. The Boy opened his eyes, deep blue irises fluttering under long lashes.

"That's him!" Pi clapped his hands and danced around the make-believe Blue. "I like this dream. Yes, I do. You're good at pretending."

"Us pretend people don't have much else to do." 62 tapped Blue's nose and he dissolved back into the familiar square block. 62 tossed the block back to Pi.

"Can you teach me how to make people from

blocks?" The younger Boy pushed and pinched the cube in his hand, but it stayed firmly in place.

"I probably can, the next time the real me sees you. If I show you now, someone might get suspicious."

Pi nodded. He blew a deep breath over the block and frowned when nothing happened.

"Hey, can you give your friend a message for me?" 62 knelt down until he was eye to eye with Pi. He wrapped his hand over the block. When he removed it the cube was gone, replaced by three spears of grass.

"Okay." Pi agreed, eyes glued to the green leaves resting in his palm.

"Please tell the Boy with blue eyes that 62 got caught by Defense. He doesn't know how he's going to get out, but he's going to try."

The smaller Boy nodded again. His eyes were somber when he looked into 62's earnest face. "I'll tell him. I hope you make it."

CHAPTER 41

Something cold and metallic poked into 62's side. A simple command was issued in a tinny voice. "Wake."

62's eyes opened cautiously and forced themselves shut again against the harsh light of the cell. One of the giant prison Machines known as Correctors stood over him. An assortment of handcuffs and keys dangled from the thing's waist. Its clamping hands opened and shut rhythmically, waiting for a reason to restrain 62. He groaned when the Corrector poked him a second time. "I hear you. I hear you. I'm up."

"You are needed in the Dream Ward. Please prepare yourself for work." The deep grinding voice of the Corrector made 62 cringe. The Machine barely fit through the opening at the mouth of the cell.

62 quickly went through his morning routine. Clean clothes and a washed face made him feel a little

better, but the optimism was lost when he opened the meal chute door and found it empty. "How long until breakfast?" No one responded.

Eventually, the door opened and 62 took that as his signal that it was time to leave. He made his way to the exit, pausing at the door to wait for one of the Correctors to fetch him. Instead, Major stood outside.

"Hello." 62 raised his cheeks in what he hoped looked to be an eager smile.

"99's report says that you were able to manipulate another being's dream."

Shrugging his shoulders, 62 kept his smile. "I guess so. I thought I was in my own dream, though."

When Major frowned, deep lines creased his face. "We've only had a couple of dreamers able to do that. They were both fully matured adults."

"Maybe they were slow learners."

The creases on Major's face deepened. "I don't like jokes."

"Okay." 62 let his smile fade. "So what do you like?"

"Results." Major turned and walked away. 62 wasn't sure if the silence that wafted behind him was an invitation to follow, so he waited in the doorway of his cell. Just before he reached the corner at the end of the hall, Major looked over and grunted. "Come on. We have work to do."

Trotting to catch up, 62 passed the Correctors. They were both in sleep mode, plugged into their housing set into the wall. There were other cell doors down this hallway, but none of the lights were on. Not that he'd ever seen much crime in Adaline, but he was surprised that he was the jail's only guest.

They made their way to the Dream Ward in

silence. Major ignored everyone they encountered, and 62 tried to balance the stiff indifference with a welcoming smile. Some Men smiled or waved in response, but most of them kept their heads down and their feet moving forward.

The door opened ahead of them when they arrived and a Nurse was already waiting to plug 62's head into the dream apparatus. 62 made his way to the bed at the end of the row cautiously. "Where's 99?"

"We don't need him for this." Major nodded to the Nurse and it placed the cap of wires on 62's head.

"But I don't know how to get to the starting point without him." 62 tried not to panic when the Nurse pushed him down on the mattress and began tying his hands to the side of the bed.

Major huffed. "You said our best dreamers might be slow learners, remember? You're probably smart enough to figure it out."

The Nurse began prattling about vitals. Major gave a thumbs up signal and then the world went dark. An aching current pressed him down into a dream. He dropped to the floor of his mind with a thud.

"Chobham." 71's voice was unmistakable. His voice repeated the password again. "Chobham. Chobham. Chobham."

"I hear you." 62 could hardly make his voice exit his throat. The pins and needles shooting through his body made measuring his speech painful.

"Chobham." 71 echoed again.

"I'm here!" He managed to shout the words despite the pain pressing in on him.

"Where's the opening? I can't see you." 71 said with concern.

"I don't think I can open it. Not yet." 62 pushed

himself up. The pain began to dull, so he moved around some more. "I'm not in a real dream."

There was a long pause. "What do you mean? You're either dreaming, or you aren't."

"71, I joined Defense like you told me to." 62 pressed his hands forward, searching for the edge of his dream. "But it's not what I thought it would be. They're hooking us to Machines and using a program to force us to dream."

"Us? There are others?" 71's voice became clearer. "Marvelous."

"No. You don't understand." 62's fingertips brushed the wall separating him from his teacher. He poked a hole in the dream and began to pull a passageway open. "They're using us to find other dreamers."

"How many more of you are there?" 71's smiling face became visible through the opening.

"Just one. My friend 1124999. You remember him?"

"Oh yes!" 71 clapped. "Such a delight that he's found his way into Defense, also. You know, I thought they'd gotten rid of the Boy. So glad to hear he's found a home after all."

"Yes, but–" 62's voice was cut off by a thumping sound from 71's side of the dream.

"What the dustdevil?" The teacher's face turned toward the sound.

"71, listen to me. They're using us to find other dreamers." The thump came again. Louder. Metallic.

"Oh?" 71's face changed from distracted curiosity to a bolt of pain. "Oh! What's going on?"

"No." 62 pushed his hand through the gap, grasping his teacher's robes. "Don't let them take you."

The light in 71's dream flickered. His face drew in

on itself as he gasped for air. "62, I don't understand. What's happening?"

"Oh, no. I'm so sorry. I didn't know this would happen!" 62 pressed his face against the gap between them. 71's robes slid between his fingers as he was being drawn away toward wakefulness. 71's light fluttered a moment more. There was a horrific crash. 71 yelled once, and then the world fell back into silence. The gap between them stitched itself up and 62 had to pull his arm back into his own dream to keep it from being caught up in the mending.

"What have I done?" 62 whispered. His dream echoed with the sound of his own crying.

CHAPTER 42

62's tears didn't stop falling when he awoke. The Nurse and Major appeared blurry and washed out as he sat up and waited for the wires to be removed from the cap atop his head. Major patted him on the back, congratulating him on his solid work. The Nurse cooed words of assurances that his body functions were normal.

"What's going to happen to him?" The words came out between hiccups. He sniffed and rubbed his nose on his sleeve.

"Happen to whom?" Major's eyes focused on the readout flowing across the screen on the computer beside the bed.

"The Man in my dream." 62 shed new tears. "He's my friend. What'll happen to him?"

"He was encouraging children to cultivate an anomaly." Major glanced at 62, turning back to his computer when their eyes met. "That's a serious offense. Treason against Adaline."

"But he loves Adaline. He wanted me to join Defense to make it better!" 62 buried his head in his hands. His tears welled between his fingers before flowing down his wrists.

"Ah, but Adaline is perfect. No improvement is needed beyond those deemed necessary by the Head Machine." Major placed a tentative hand on the Boy's shoulder. "You helped us to close a very disruptive loop in the system. This is the work you were designed for."

"No." 62 shook his head. "No no no. I'm an anomaly. I wasn't designed this way. It was a mistake. This was all a mistake."

Major considered the Boy for a moment. "Perhaps. But it's a happy mistake. Now we move forward. On to find the next bug to be fixed."

62 looked up at Major, eyes already bloodshot from his tears. He wiped his runny nose again with his sleeve. "You still haven't told me what will happen to him."

"He'll be given the same choice you were given. Help us to remove other anomalies, or be removed himself."

"He'll never help you." 62 whispered.

"Are you sure?" Major removed his hand and folded his arms with a smirk. "You said yourself that he wanted you to join Defense. Had we known that he may be sympathetic to our cause, we would have tried harder to find him a long time ago."

"He – he wants to give us the freedom to dream." 62's hiccups prevented him from sounding as angry as he felt.

"For what purpose?" Major scoffed. "It's a waste of time. Inhibits rest, reduces the ability to follow clear directions and opens up ideas for debate where none is needed."

"You're wrong." 62 growled. "About all of it."

Major squatted down beside the bed. He placed his hands on either side of 62 on the mattress. He looked the Boy square in the eye, jaw clenched and eyes alight with fire. "Your friend will help us, or he will die."

62 threw himself at Major, kicking and screaming at the top of his lungs. He careened over the Man's shoulder, pulling his hair as he fell down his backside. Major stood up, flailing his arms around 62 and turning in circles to get him off. The Nurse grabbed at them both. Her hands locked onto one of 62's feet and one of his hands just before they came crashing down on Major once more.

"You're going to get it, you little sneak!" Major howled as 62 bit his arm. The Nurse and Major together pulled 62 to the floor, pinning him down. "Nurse. Sedate him!"

A needle protruded from one of the Nurse's busy fingers, pricking through the skin of 62's thigh. A cool tingle spread from the tiny wound. It filled his leg and moved into the rest of his body with rapid speed. "I won't let you do this!" 62 cried. "You can't take us. You can't!"

For the second time that cycle, the darkness was forced onto 62's mind. This time, there were no dreams.

CHAPTER 43

"Wake." The familiar poke of a metal boot pressed against 62's side.

"You don't need to step on me." 62 rolled over to face the giant Machine that towered over him. "I wasn't asleep."

The Machine backed out of the cell and a much shorter shadow appeared in the doorway. A person entered and sat down just inside the door. The Machine locked it shut behind him. It took a moment for 62's eyes to adjust to the light that flickered on overhead. When he blinked the sting of the fluorescents away, 99 looked back at him.

"It's been a few cycles since you've worked in the Dream Ward." 99 stated the fact as if 62 wasn't aware that he'd refused to exit his cell at Major's beckoning.

"What did they do to 71?" 62 tried to read emotion on his brother's face, but there was none.

"He's being tested."

62 rolled over to face the far wall. He didn't know what it meant for 71 to be tested, but whether he was succumbing to forced dreams in the ward or being poked at in a lab made no difference. He pulled the blanket over his face.

"The least you can do is come help him find his way." 99 prodded. "Maybe if he saw you, he would be encouraged to help us. The way you felt when you saw me."

"You tricked me." 62 spat the words into his blanket. The thin fabric did nothing to filter the anger in his voice.

"I didn't trick you," 99 offered. "I didn't even know you."

62 pushed himself off the floor, ready for a fight. He glared at the Boy who had once been his closest brother, seething in anger. "You knew what they would do to me. What they'd do to my friends. And still you helped them to find us. To hunt us down like bugs in faulty software."

99 nodded. "That's what you are, really. Fleshy bits out of place."

"No." 62's hands balled into fists. "We're more than fleshy bits. And who are you to determine whether or not we're out of place? You and I are the same. We have the same anomaly. The same dreams. If I'm a bug in the system, then what are you?"

"Major says I'm the fix. The patch to make the world run smoothly again." 99 shrugged. "You could hold the same power, if you'd just come back to the ward."

"You don't even report everyone!" 62's fists pounded the wall beside him, his frustration too much to bear. Each hit produced a clang in the hollow metal wall. "We went past so many dreamers, ones you didn't even look at because you are too afraid to be alone."

"I report what's needed. Pi, for example, will someday be pulled into the ward. For now, he's far more useful in the Nursery. If we remove him, how will we know what the bad people are up to?"

62 gritted his teeth. "They aren't bad. And even if they do break the rules, they're nowhere near as bad as you."

99 looked surprised. "I'm a good Boy. I follow all instructions given to me without question."

It was like talking to a Machine. The light of intelligence was washed from 99's eyes. He was no longer the friend that 62 remembered, and hadn't been since the cycle he turned himself in as defective. 62 growled, "Well, I have questions."

"Then you have doubts that what we're doing is best for Adaline."

"I have no doubts. This is wrong. You are wrong."

99 gave a slight nod. "I'll let Major know you've made your decision then."

"It doesn't matter what 71 decides to do." 62 shook his head. "I'm not helping you anymore."

The Boy who 62 had loved above all others rose from his corner of the room. 99 gave another sharp nod, then pressed his hand to the door. The cell door opened, 99 exited, and 62 fell back to the floor. Tears streamed down his face. It wasn't the first time he'd been singled out because of his actions, but never before had he felt so alone.

CHAPTER 44

It wasn't long before someone in a lab coat came for him. 62 stood, determined to not be afraid. The Man looked wary of him, as if touching him might pass along a disease. 62 followed the Man out of the cell and into the hall. Maybe dreams were a disease. But they were also wonderful and amazing in ways that he'd never find words to describe.

"This way." The Man tilted his head to the left. The motion was unnecessary, since two of the correction bots grabbed 62's arms and pushed him down the hallway behind the swishing tails of the lab coat.

Through the booking office and out into the main corridor of Defense, 62 was pushed as far away from all of the healthy and productive workers as possible. The Man in the lab coat stopped in front of an elevator, pushing the up button six times in rapid succession as if it would make the gears turn faster.

62, the Correctors and the Man squeezed into the

tiny box once the elevator doors finally opened. The Man gave 62 a weary look as he pushed the button for Level 2.

"I haven't been up that high before." 62 commented.

The Man gave 62 a sideways glance. "Not many have."

"What do they do there?"

The Man took a step closer to the door. A shrug of his shoulders the only answer. 62 nodded. The elevator rose quickly, sending 62's feet into the floor. It felt like all of the blood was going to rush out of him through his toes. A ridiculous thought. 62 gave a smirk. When the elevator dinged and the door slid open, there was an uncomfortable jostle between Man and Machine as they worked out who would exit the narrow door first. The lab coat won the dance, and flitted out ahead of the rest of the group.

"To prep." The Man pointed the Machines down a hallway past a series of offices. The lights were different up here. Yellower than in the levels where 62 lived. The fixtures seemed older. Switches coated in the gray-brown film of too many fingers and not enough cleaners. The floors covered in bumpy carpet with depressions and stains in patterns that suggested that the furniture in each passing room had once been somewhere else.

The Correctors forced 62 to stop at an oversized steel door. Tings and shuffles could be heard just behind it, suggesting someone lived just beyond the heavy metal barrier. The Corrector on his right reached forward, pressing its finger to a data pad. A whirring of locks unlatching was followed by a low squeal. Another Man in an older lab coat waited just inside.

"1124562," the Man said, reading from his tablet. "So good of you to join us."

The Correctors retreated, the slab of a door swung shut, and 62 stared at the Man with as much courage as he could muster. "What's going to happen to me?"

"We're going to do some tests." The Man's sly grin made 62's stomach turn. "That will determine what will happen next."

Despite his fluttering heart and the twisting of his stomach, the tests involved nothing more than a scanner placed against his neck. Data passed through the scanner and onto the Man's pad. He made a series of sighs and snorts as information filled his screen.

"Disappointing," said the Man in the threadbare lab coat. He stepped over to the wall behind him and opened a small hatch, no larger than the books 62 sometimes read in his dreams. "Everything is in order. No anomalies to report aside from the dreams. Sadly, no dissections today."

62 could hear a Nurse in the next room come to life. Instruments clanged against metal drawers as it began putting things away. 62 let go of a breath he hadn't realized he'd been holding, his worst fear avoided by way of his hacked chip.

"What now?" 62 asked quietly.

The doctor shrugged. "Disposal, of course. Anomalies must be removed from Adaline."

The Man tapped his tablet, calling a pair of Transportation Aides. When the wide steel door opened, they waited just outside with a gurney in tow. The Aide closest to 62 reached out to grab him, but he ducked under the outstretched arm and ran past the Machine. He tore down the hall toward the elevator, but the Correctors hadn't yet left and they rushed toward him when he drew near. Pinned between the Transportation Aides and

Correctors, he ducked into a side office and locked the flimsy brown door.

Three knocks sounded and a muffled voice found its way through. "Come out, now. This floor isn't designed for little ones. Open the door before you get hurt."

"What is disposal?" 62 shouted back.

There was a long pause before the voice answered. "I'm sorry. Your anomaly isn't one we can repair. We have to remove you from the system."

"But what does that mean?" 62 screamed.

"Just open the door."

62 ignored the Man. There wasn't any way out of the room, but he wouldn't let them in to get him. A desk and chair sat in the center of the room. 62 tucked himself underneath, out of sight of the jiggling door handle.

A moment later he heard the click of the latch. The hinges swung quietly but the knob bumped the wall when the door opened fully. 62 watched a pair of shoes walk across the carpet, around the desk and stop behind the chair. "I'm sorry," was all the shoes had to say.

CHAPTER 45

62 wiggled his toes in protest as the Transportation Aides pushed him down a long hallway. Gone were the flickering yellow lights, replaced with overpowering white bars of illumination that made the quick moving Machines gleam. The gurney stopped rolling when it approached a group of patients waiting just outside a large metal door.

The door had no window or handle. It was set into the wall between wide steel panels that held hundreds of thick rivets. The Aides loosened the straps around 62's hands and feet, but held him tight by his forearms to keep him from running again as they guided him into line.

The others who waited at the door were solemn. Most didn't even look up as 62 and his custodians approached. There were Men. Boys. Small fidgeting toddlers. Two babies squealed in the arms of red-eyed Nannies.

A robotic head eased down from the ceiling. One singular red eye scanned the group. A high-pitched melodic voice chimed from above. "Hello. Thank you for participating in Adaline. I regret to inform you that you have acquired an anomaly that cannot be repaired. Please, be a good citizen and enter the containment area."

Long segmented arms reached out from the gantry. The curved grip of their hands clipped at the air above the people's heads, waiting for someone to disobey. The Transportation Aides released their hold. The large metal door opened with a whine that rang in 62's ears and he was thankful that he had use of his arms again so he could cover them.

When the door hung open, 62 dropped his hands with a gasp. "I know this place."

"Improbable." The red eyed orb moved toward 62 and chirped. "This location is for biological disposal only. You are not authorized to operate this device."

The arms gripped 62's shoulders and pushed him forward. His feet tried to grip the floor, but the slick tile only squeaked beneath his toes. The other Boys and Men shuffled forward, entering the metal box without protest. But 62 had seen this place before when he shared a dream with the doctor from Level 2. In the dream, flames shot out from just inside the doorway. Now, as he was being pushed into the gaping opening, it lay quiet and unassuming. But he knew the fate that awaited him.

"No!" 62 shouted. He tried to pull the claw-like arms off of his shoulders, but they only tightened their grasp. "I'm not unwell! My anomaly can be fixed. I can be a good Boy."

"Thank you for cooperating." The red eye peered down at him as it continued to guide him into the room. It pushed him past the younger Boys near the door, toward a side wall. The vice-like grip forced him down onto a bench coated in black silt.

62 wept as the Machine strapped a belt around his waist, preventing him from rushing the door. Small, spindly bots with long, wiry arms skittered across the room, buckling the others down. The deep red eye of the Machine that tightened 62's strap cooed, "Too tight?"

62 screamed in response.

The disposal Machine backed out of the door, waving a claw in farewell. The smaller bots collided with one another as they raced out of the closing door. The babies cried, their voices mingling in the air with 62's screams. Men and Boys looked worried, but remained silent. Obedient.

They were all doomed to die.

CHAPTER 46

62 closed his eyes in fear of the flames he remembered from the doctor's dream. He held his breath, waiting for the oxygen to be sucked from his lungs. He waited, crying and trembling in the dark until he couldn't hold his breath any longer.

A slight click was heard toward the back of the room, and he felt warm air rush past his face. He braced himself against the wall, anticipating the shooting pain of his final moments. Every muscle stung as it strained against his restraints.

Between the babies' cries from across the room, 62 heard a snicker. "Don't worry. I ain't gonna bite."

62 eased an eye open. A low hatch at the back of the room was wedged open. Air flowed from the small gap in the metal wall near the place 62 was strapped to the bench. Light streamed in around a Boy's upside-down head, turning his hair gold and putting his face in shadow.

"What's going on?" A Man's nervous voice called out.

"Who are you?" 62 asked. The babies cried louder.

The Boy scrambled in, flicking on a portable light strapped to his shoulder. "You don't even recognize your old friend, Blue?" The Boy moved swiftly, undoing the restraint around 62's waist.

"What are you doing here?" 62 was exasperated, his voice coming in a shout of emotion. A stream of Boys flowed in through the open hatch. The quiet click of unbuckled straps repeated in 62's ear.

Blue covered 62's mouth and pulled him off the bench. "Shhhh. Not so loud. This box may be fireproof, but it sure ain't soundproof." He waited for everyone to be unstrapped and standing. "Now everybody scream a little. Make it sound like we're cutting your legs off."

62 stood in the center of the dark box. "Aaaaaahhh."

A few other voices moaned with him. The babies wailed and the Boys holding them moved closer to the hatch. Blue turned from where he was re-strapping the belt to the bench. "Come on. You all can do better than that."

"AAAAAAAAAHHHHHHHHH!" Everyone yelled in agony. A chorus of despair. The Men's voices drowned out the crying babies.

Blue winked. "That's the stuff. Keep going."

All of the Boys who had come in through the hatched worked in a flurry. They dumped soot onto the benches where the prisoners sat a moment before. They dipped their hands in the mess and spread hand prints over the walls.

Blue moved behind 62, pulled out a blade and cut

into his neck.

"OOOWW!" 62 spun around to find Blue grinning, holding his chip between the fingers of the hand not holding a scalpel. All around him, the others did the same.

Blue tossed the chip into the soot, waved his hand toward the hatch, and everyone began climbing through. The light was blinding. It was warm in a way that 62 had never felt before. He crawled away from the large metal box, shielding his eyes with one hand and groping through the dirt with the other. Blades of grass wove their way through his fingers.

62 stopped. He sat on his haunches and forced his eyes to focus in the bright light that seemed to be coming from everywhere. Someone bumped into him from behind and he scooted forward a few more yards. Grass padded his knees and the thin blades were unexpectedly sharp between his fingers. Dozens of other bodies bounded through a field just ahead. Blue turned, looking for 62.

"Come on!" Blue shouted as he ran back to where 62 sat, dumbstruck by his surroundings. "You kids are always so stupid when you come out of that box. We've got to get out of here before one of those patrol bots comes by this side of the building."

62 looked up and saw the fence where some of the others were standing, waving their arms and shouting for those still in the field to hurry. Blue grabbed 62 by the tunic and pulled him to his feet, urging him on again. "Let's go, dummy."

Adrenaline pumped through 62's veins. "This isn't a dream?"

"No. Those bots are real as anything, and they're going to check on us any minute." Blue looked over his shoulder and waved at the others to go on without them.

"I'm not dead?"

"Not yet." Blue grinned.

"Okay. I'm ready." 62's feet started moving toward the fence at the far end of the field. The long grass slapped against his legs as he ran. The sun beat down on his bare neck, making the cut on his neck sting with heat and sweat. He reached the fence and turned around, wanting one quick glance of Adaline from outside.

The structure loomed over the overgrown lawn. Its sharp lines were broken by orderly panes of glass, spread out across the building. It looked tattered and forgotten, worn beyond repair. And yet, so many lives were spread out inside of it. "Not inside." 62 whispered. "Below."

Something metallic gleamed around the corner. 62 gasped when Blue tugged his tunic. He spun on his heel and dove through a gap in the diamond-patterned fence, then helped Blue push the wire back into place so it looked like one continuous panel again.

"This way." Blue urged before diving down into a ditch. 62 followed. He ducked below the protection of green plants. Sun dotted his skin from overhead. The air moved all around him, filling his lungs and whispering for him to keep going. It wasn't a dream. He was outside, and it was more real than anything he'd ever known.

ABOUT THE AUTHOR

Denise Kawaii is the author of a growing variety of books and novelettes. She is a long-time resident of the Pacific Northwest, moving periodically between Oregon and Washington State as the mood suits her. When not writing books, Denise plays at being a farmer. Currently wrapped up in the interesting practice of vermicomposting, she feeds her worm bin a mixture of kitchen scraps and negative reviews.

A woman of many talents, Kawaii also writes fiction for grown-ups under the pen name D.K. Greene. Her crime fiction novel, *S is for Serial*, and other varied works can be found on her website, www.KawaiiTimes.com.

Made in the USA
San Bernardino, CA
11 April 2017